BEST LAID SCHEMES

TO
WILL H. HAYS
WHOSE FRIENDSHIP IS MORE TO BE PRIZED
THAN MUCH FINE GOLD

CONTENTS

PAGE

THE SUSINESS OF SUSAN 3

THE GIRL WITH THE RED FEATHER . . . 34

THE CAMPBELLS ARE COMING 74

ARABELLA'S HOUSE PARTY 115

THE THIRD MAN 167

WRONG NUMBER 197

BEST LAID SCHEMES

THE SUSINESS OF SUSAN

I

SUSAN PARKER was twenty-six and nothing had ever happened. To speak more accurately, plenty of things had happened, but Man had never happened. As a college girl and afterward, Susie had, to be sure, known many men; but they had all passed by on the other side. A young man of literary ambitions had once directed a sonnet at Susie, but she was not without critical judgment and she knew it for a weak effort. This young man afterward became the sporting editor of a great newspaper, and but for Susie's fastidiousness in the matter of sonnets she might have shared his prosperity and fame. A professor of theology had once sent her a sermon on the strength of a chance meeting at a tea; but this, though encouraging, was hardly what might be called a thrilling incident. Still, the young professor had later been called to an important church, and a little more enthusiasm for sermons on Susie's part might have changed the current of her life.

The brother of one of Susie's Vassar classmates had evinced a deep interest in Susie for a few months, spending weekends at Poughkeepsie that might much better have been devoted to working off his conditions at New Haven; but the frail argosy of their young affections had gone to smash with incredible ease and swiftness over a careless assertion by Susie that, after

3

all, Harvard was the greatest American university.
All universities looked alike to her, and she had really
been no more interested in Harvard than in the aca-
demic centers of Wyoming or Oklahoma. Now this
young gentleman was launched successfully as a mining engineer and had passed Susan by for another of
his sister's classmates, who was not nearly so interesting
or amusing as Susie.

Susie's mother had died while she was in college,
and her father, in the year she was graduated. As he
had chosen a good name rather than great riches,
Susie had found it necessary to adjust herself to conditions, which she did by taking the library course at
Witter Institute. In Syracuse, where Susan was born,
old friends of the family had said how fortunate it was
that her education made library work possible for her.
And, though this was true, Susie resented their tone
of condescension. In its various implications it dis-
missed her from the world to which she had been
accustomed to another and very different sphere. It
meant that if she became an attendant in the Syracuse
Library she would assist at no more teas, and that
gradually she would be forgotten in the compilations
of lists of eligibles for such functions as illuminate the
social horizon of Syracuse.

Whereupon, being a duly accredited librarian, entitled to consideration as such wherever book ware-
houses exist, Susan decided to try her luck in a strange
land, where hours from nine to six would be less heartbreaking than in a town where every one would say
how brave Susie was, or how shameful it was that her
father had not at least kept up his life insurance.

The archives of Denver, Omaha and Indianapolis

beckoned. She chose Indianapolis as being nearer the ocean.

In her changes of status and habitat the thing that hurt Susan most was the fact that the transition fixed her, apparently for all time, among the Susans. She had been named Susan for an aunt with money, but the money had gone to foreign missions when Susie was six. In college she had always been Susie to those who did not call her Miss Parker. Her introduction to the library in the Hoosier capital was, of course, as Miss Parker; but she saw Miss Susan looming darkly ahead of her. She visualized herself down the gray vistas, preyed upon daily by harassed women in search of easy catercorners to club papers, who would ask at the counter for Miss Susan. And she resented, with all the strength of her healthy young soul, the thought of being Miss Susan.

Just why Sue and Susie express various shades of character and personal atmosphere not hinted in the least by Susan pertains to the psychology of names, and is not for this writing. Susie was a small human package with a great deal of yellow hair, big blue eyes, an absurdly small mouth and a determined little nose. As a child and throughout her college years she had been frolicsome and prankish. Her intimates had rejected Sue as an inappropriate diminutive for her. Sue and Susie are not interchangeable. Sue may be applied to tall, dark girls; but no one can imagine a Susie as tall or dark. In college the girls had by unanimous consent called her Susie, with an affectionate lingering upon the second syllable and a prolongation of the "e."

To get exactly the right effect, one should first bite

Mrs. Burgess was to follow at once, accompanied by her younger sister, Miss Wilkinson; and that she was to entertain immediately Mr. Brown Pendleton, a wealthy young American explorer and archæologist, who was coming to Indiana to deliver the dedicatory address at the opening of the new Historical Museum at the state university. Mrs. Burgess always entertained all the distinguished people who visited Indianapolis, and it had occurred to Susan that by the exercise of ordinary vigilance she might catch a glimpse of Brown Pendleton during his stay at the house next door. Webster Burgess was a banker who had inherited his bank, and he had always found life rather pleasant going. His wife diverted him a good deal, and the fact that she played at being a highbrow amused him almost more than anything else. He had kept his figure, and at forty-two was still able to dance without fear of apoplexy. He chose his haberdashery with taste, and sometimes he sent flowers to ladies without inclosing his wife's card; but his wife said this was temperamental, which was a very good name for it.

Susie, holding her ground as Burgess advanced, composedly patted the head of one of the bronze lions that guarded the entrance to the Logan doors.

"Good evening! It's mighty nice to see you back again," said Burgess, smiling.

It was at this instant that Susan, hearing the god of adventure sounding the call to arms, became Susie again.

"I'm very glad to see you, Mr. Burgess," she replied; and ceasing to fondle the bronze lion's left ear she gave the banker her hand. "Summer is hanging on," observed Susie; "it's quite warm this evening."

"It is, indeed, and most of our neighbors seem to be staying away late; but I'm glad you're back."

Susie was glad he was back. Her superficial knowledge of Mr. Webster Burgess bore wholly upon his standing as a banker. In the year she had spent in his ancestral city she had never heard anything to justify a suspicion that he was a gentleman given to flirtations with strange young women. There was something quite cozy and neighborly in his fashion of addressing her. His attitude seemed paternal rather than otherwise. He undoubtedly mistook her for a member of the Logan household. It crossed her mind that he probably knew little of the Logan family, who had occupied the new house only to leave it; but she knew there were several Logan girls, for she was occupying the room designed for one of them.

"This is what I call downright good luck!" Burgess continued, glancing at his watch. "Mrs. Burgess reaches town at six, with her sister—and Brown Pendleton, the explorer, and so on. We met him at Little Boar's Head, and you know how Mrs. Burgess is—she wanted to be sure he saw this town right. A mighty interesting chap—his father left him a small mint, and he spends his income digging. He's dug up about all the Egyptians, Babylonians and Ninevites. He's coming out to make a speech—thinks of prying into the mound-builders; though I don't see why any one should. Do you?"

"On the whole I think the idea rather tickles me," said Susie. "I always thought it would be fun to try a lid-lifter on the dead past."

Mr. Burgess took note of her anew and chuckled.

"Open up kings like sardines! I like your way of putting it."

"A few canned kings for domestic consumption," added Susie, thinking that he was very easy to talk to. The fact that he did not know her from a daughter of the royal house of Rameses made not the slightest difference now that the adventurous spirit of the old Susie days possessed her.

Mr. Burgess was scrutinizing the telegram again.

"I want you to dine with us this evening—as a special favor, you know. It's rather sudden, but Mrs. Burgess has a sudden way of doing things. Just as I left my office I got this wire ordering me to produce the most presentable girl I could find for dinner. Pendleton hates big functions, but I nailed Billy Merrill at the club on my way up, according to instructions— you can always get Billy; but I went through the telephone book without finding any unattached woman of suitable age I would dare take a shot at, knowing my wife's prejudices. And then I looked over here and saw you."

His manner conveyed, with the utmost circumspection, the idea that seeing her had brightened the world considerably.

"Certainly, Mr. Burgess," replied Susie, without the slightest hesitation or qualm. "At seven, did you say?"

"Seven-thirty we'd better say. There's my machine and I've got to go to the station to meet them."

As Susan, the thing would have been impossible; as Susie, it seemed the most natural thing in the world. Burgess was backing down the steps. Every instant reduced the possibility of retreat; but the fact was, that she exulted in her sin. She was an impostor and she rejoiced shamelessly in being an impostor. And yet it did not seem altogether square to accept Mr. Burgess' invitation to dinner when it would undoubtedly involve him in difficulties with his wife, whom she had never seen in her life.

Burgess paused and wheeled round abruptly.

Her Susiness experienced a shock—the incident, in her hasty conjecture, was already closed—for he said:

"By-the-way, what is your name anyhow?"

"Susie," she said, lifting her chin Susily.

Mr. Burgess laughed, as though it were perfectly obvious that she was a Susie—as though any one at a glance ought to know that this young person in the white flannel skirt and blue shirt-waist was a Susie, ordained to be so called from the very first hour of creation.

"Just for fun, what's the rest of it?" he asked.

"Parker, please. I'm not even a poor relation of the Logans."

"I didn't suppose you were; quite and distinctly not!" he declared as though the Logans were wholly obnoxious. "I never saw you before in my life—did I?"

"Never," said Susie, giving him the benefit of her blue eyes.

Burgess rubbed his ear reflectively.

"I think I'm in for a row," he remarked in an agreeable tone, as though rows of the sort he had in mind were not distasteful to him.

"Of course," said Susie with an air of making concessions, "if you really didn't mean to ask me to dinner, or have changed your mind now that you find I'm a stranger and a person your wife would never invite to her house, we'll call the party off."

"Heavens, no! You can't send regrets to a dinner at the last minute. And if you don't show up I'm going to be in mighty bad. You see——" He gazed at Susie with the keen scrutiny he reserved for customers when they asked to have their lines of credit extended, and he carefully weighed the moral risk. "We seem to be on amazingly intimate terms, considering our short acquaintance. There's something about you that inspires confidence."

"I'm much uplifted by this tribute," said Susie with a Susesque touch that escaped her so naturally, so easily, that she marveled at herself.

Burgess smiled broadly.

"I'm afraid," he remarked, "that you don't quite fill the bill; but you'll do—you've got to do!"

He handed her the telegram he had retained in his hand and watched her face as she read:

> P. is greatly taken with Floy, and we must give her every chance. Pick up an uninteresting young man and one of the least attractive of the older girls for dinner tonight. This is important. Make no mistake.

"Those are my instructions. Can you ever forgive me?"

"With my hair brushed straight back, they say I'm quite homely," observed Susie sighing.

"I shouldn't do my worst," said the banker, "where Nature has been so generous."

"It seems," observed Susie meditatively, "that I'm your deliberate choice as a foil for your sister-in-law, by sheer force of my unattractiveness."

"I'm slightly nearsighted," replied the banker. "It's a frightful handicap."

"I can see that glasses would be unbecoming to you."

"The matter of eyes," said the banker, stroking a lion, "is not one I should trust myself to discuss with you. Do you mind telling me what you're doing here?"

"Cutting the leaves in the books and making a card catalogue. I use the typewriter with a dexterity that has been admired."

"A person of education, clearly."

"French and German were required by my college; and I speak English with only a slight Onondaga accent, as you observe."

Her essential Susiness seemed to be communicating itself to the banker. His chauffeur loosened a raucous blast of the horn warningly.

"I fear your time is wasted. The Logans will never read those books. It's possible that the hand of Fate guided me across the lawn to deliver you from the lions. The thought pleases me. To continue our confidences, I will say that, noble woman though my wife is, her sister has at times annoyed me. And when I left Little Boar's Head I saw that Pendleton suspected that we were trying to kidnap him."

"And I take it that the natural fellow-feeling of man for man would mitigate your sorrow if the gentleman whom your wife is carrying home in a birdcage should not, in fact, become your brother-in-law."

"It would be indelicate for me to go so far as that; but Floy has always had a snippy way with me. I should like to see her have to work for the prize."

"My dinner frock is three years old, but I'll see what I can do to become a natural hazard. You'd better move upon the station—the blasts of that horn are not soothing to the nerves."

III

Brown Pendleton, Ph.D., L.H.D., F.R.G.S., frowned as he adjusted his white tie before the mirror of the Burgesses' best guest-room. He was a vigorous, healthy American of thirty, quite capable of taking care of himself; and yet he had been dragged submissively across the continent by a lady who was animated by an ambition to marry him to her sister, toward whom his feelings, in the most minute self-analysis, were only those of polite indifference. And the mound-builders, now that he thought of it, were rather tame after Egypt and Babylon. As he surveyed his tanned face above his snowy shirt bosom he wished that he had never consented to deliver the address at the opening of the new Historical Museum at Indiana University, which was the ostensible reason for this Western flight. As for Miss Floy Wilkinson, she was a perfectly conventional person, who had—not to be more explicit—arrived at a time of life when people say of a girl that she is holding her own well. And she was. She was indubitably handsome, but not exciting. She was the sort of girl who makes an ideal house guest, and she had walked down church aisles ahead of one after the other of her old school friends all the way from Duluth to Bangor. Mrs. Burgess had become anxious as to Floy's future, and in convoying Pendleton to Indianapolis and planting him in her best guest-chamber she was playing her cards with desperation.

Mrs. Burgess ran upstairs to dress after a hasty cross-examination of the cook, to make sure her telegraphic order for dinner had been understood, and found her husband shaking himself into his dress coat.

She presented her back to be unhooked and talked on in a way she had.

"Well, I suppose you got Grace Whiting or Minnie Rideout? And, of course, you couldn't have failed on Billy Merrill. I think Grace and Billy are showing signs, at last, of being interested in each other. You can't tell what may have happened during the summer. But if Pendleton should fail—well, Billy isn't so dull as people think; and Floy doesn't mind his clumsiness so much as she did. Did you say you got Minnie?"

Mr. Burgess, absorbed in a particularly stubborn hook, was silent. Mrs. Burgess was afraid to urge conversation upon him lest he should throw up the job, and Floy was monopolizing the only available maid. When a sigh advertised his triumph over the last hook she caught him as he was moving toward the door.

"Did you say Minnie was coming, Web?"

"No, Gertie—no. You didn't say anything about Minnie in your telegram; you said to get a girl."

"Why, Web, you know that meant Grace Whiting or Minnie Rideout; they are my old standbys."

"Well, Grace has gone somewhere to bury her uncle, and Minnie is motoring through the Blue Grass. It was pretty thin picking, but I did the best I could."

His tone and manner left much to be desired. His wife's trunk was being unstrapped in the hall outside and there was no time for parleying.

"Whom did you get, then? Not——"

"I got Susie," said Burgess, shooting his cuffs.

"Susie?"

"Susie!" he repeated with falling inflection.

"What Susie?"

"Well, Gertie, to be quite frank, I'll be hanged if I know. I haven't the slightest, not the remotest, idea."

"What do you mean, Web?—if you know!"

The clock on the stairs below was chiming half past six. Burgess grinned; it was not often he had a chance like this. In social affairs it was she who did the befuddling.

"I mean to say that, though her name is Susie, it's rather more than a proper name; it's also a common

ance she related an anecdote, at which the guest of
honor only smiled wanly. He did not seem happy.
He barely tasted his soup, and when Burgess addressed
a question to him directly Pendleton did not hear it
until it had been repeated. Things were not going
well. Then Billy Merrill asked Pendleton if he was
related to some Pendletons he knew in St. Louis.
Almost every one knew that Brown Pendleton belonged to an old Rhode Island family—and Merrill
should have known it. Mrs. Burgess was enraged by
the fleeting grin she detected on her husband's face.
Web was always so unsympathetic. Burgess was con-
versing tranquilly with Susie; he never grasped the
idea that his wife gave small dinners to encourage general conversation. And this strange girl would not
contribute to the conversation; she seemed to be making curious remarks to Webster in a kind of baby talk
that made him choke with mirth. "An underbred,
uncultivated person!" thought Mrs. Burgess.

Mrs. Burgess decided that it would not be amiss to
take soundings in the unknown's past and immediate
present.

"You don't usually come back to town so early, do
you, Miss Parker?" she asked sweetly.

"No; but Newport was rather slow this year—so
many of the houses weren't open."

Mrs. Burgess and her sister exchanged a glance of
startled surprise. Brown Pendleton's thoughts came
back from Babylon. Merrill looked at Miss Parker
with open-eyed admiration.

"Dear old Newport!" Pendleton remarked with feeling. "It has rather lost tone. I'm not surprised that
you didn't care for it."

He examined Susie with deliberation.

"The Niedlingers and the Parquetries didn't show

up at all; and the Ossingtons are said to have cut it
out for good," observed Susie.

"Yes; I saw Fred Ossington in London in the spring,
and he said he had enough.   Nice chap, Fred."

"Too bad he had to give up polo," said Susie, advancing her pickets daringly; "but I fancy his arm will
never be fit again."

"He's going in for balloons.   Can you believe it?
Amusing fellow!   Said he preferred falling on the earth
to having it fall on him.   And, besides, a balloon
couldn't kick when it had him down."

The conversation was picking up, and quite clearly
it was the unknown who was giving it momentum.
Fish had been disposed of satisfactorily and Mrs. Burgess began to regain confidence.   The unknown must
be checked.   It would not do for the girl to go further
with this light, casual discussion, conveying as she did
all sorts of implications of knowledge of the great in
lofty places.   The vintage of the dinner gown testified
unimpeachably against her having any real knowledge
of Newport, a place where Mrs. Burgess had once
spent a day at a hotel.   Mrs. Burgess resolved to
squelch the impostor.   Such presumption should not
go unrebuked even at one's own table.   Pendleton
was now discussing aviation with this impertinent
Susie, who brought to the subject the same light
touch of apparent sophistication she had employed
in speaking of Newport and polo.   She asked him if
he had read an account of a new steering device for
dirigibles; she thought she had seen it in *L'Illustration*.
Pendleton was interested, and scribbled the approxi-
mate date of the journal on the back of his namecard.

"I suppose you came back ahead of your family,
Miss Parker?   I really don't know who's in town."

"Yes; I'm quite alone, Mrs. Burgess.   You see,"

Every one says that your 'Brickyards of Nebuchadnezzar' is the last word on that subject."

And then a chill seized Mrs. Burgess. The yellow-
haired, blue-eyed unknown moved her head slightly to
one side, bit an almond in two with neatness, and said:

"If I were you, Mr. Pendleton, I shouldn't let a
faker like Geisendanner annoy me."

Susie regarded the remaining half of the almond
indifferently and then ate it musingly. At the mention of Geisendanner Pendleton flushed, and his head
lifted as though he heard trumpets calling to action.
Then he bent toward Susie. The salad had just been
removed. Mrs. Burgess beat the table with her fingers
and awaited the earthquake. Her only relief at the
moment was in the consciousness that her husband,
from the look of his face, at last realized the heinousness
of his conduct in bringing just any little whipper-
snapper to her table. And Susie seemed to be the
only member of the company who was wholly tranquil.
Mrs. Burgess wondered whether she could be more
than twenty, so complete had been the reinvestiture of
the girl in the robes of her Susiness. She had spoken
of Geisendanner as though he lived round the corner
and were a person that every one with any sort of
decent bringing up knew or should know. The effect
of the name upon Pendleton was not pleasant to see,
and Mrs. Burgess shuddered. After the first shock of
surprise he seemed wonderfully subdued. Clearly this
Geisendanner was an enemy or a man he feared. The
eminent Babylonian met Susie's eyes apprehensively.
He said in a low tone of dejection:

"So you know then?" As though of course she did,
and that a dark understanding had thus been established by their common knowledge.

Susie nodded.

"Rather absurd, on the whole, when you consider
———"

Her plate was being changed and she drew back
during the interruption. Pendleton shook his head
impatiently at the delay.

"Absurd! How absurd? If it's absurd to have the
results of years of hard work chucked into the rubbish
heap, then———"

"But no!" Susie felt for her fork without breaking
the contact of their eyes. She was smiling as though
quite the mistress of the occasion and waiting merely
to prolong the agony of the sufferers about her. She
was not insensible to their sufferings; it was pleasant
rather than otherwise to inflict torture. Still her attitude toward the distressed scientist was kindly—but
she would make him wait. Her bearing toward Pendleton at the moment was slightly maternal. It was
only a matter of bricks anyhow; and trifles like the
chronological arrangement of bricks, where, one top-
pling, all went down, were not only to the young person's liking but quite within the range of her powers of
manipulation. "As I remember," she continued, "Geisendanner first attacked the results of the Deutsche
Orientgesellschaft; but, of course, that was disposed of."

"Yes," assented Pendleton eagerly; "Auchengloss did
that."

It seemed preposterous that the small mouth of this
young person could utter such names at all, much less
with an air of familiarity, as though they were the
names of streets or of articles of commerce.

"It was Glosbrenner, however, who paved the way
for you by disposing of Geisendanner—absolutely."

"The excavations they made in their absurd search

for treasure in the ruins confused everything; but Glosbrenner's exposé was lost—burnt up in a printing-office
fire in Berlin.   There's not an assertion in my 'Brickyards of Nebuchadnezzar' that isn't weakened by that
bronze-gate rubbish, for Geisendanner was a scholar of
some reputation.   After the failure of his hidden-
treasure scheme he faked his book on the Bronze Gates
of Babylon as a pot boiler, and died leaving it behind
him—one of the most plausible frauds ever perpetrated.   They went in on top of my excavations of the
brickyard—thought because I was an American I
must have been looking for gold images.   Glosbrenner
was an American student; and seeing that his fellow-
adventurer's book was taken seriously he wrote his
exposé, swore to it before the American consul at
Berlin and then started for Tibet to sell an automobile
to the Grand Lama—and never came back."

Pendleton's depression had increased; gloom settled
upon the company—or upon all but this demure young
skeleton at the feast, who had thus outrageously
brought to the table the one topic of all topics in the
world that was the most ungrateful to the man Mrs.
Burgess most particularly wished to please.   She sought
without avail to break in upon a dialogue that excluded
the rest of the company as completely as though they
were in the kitchen.

"I was just reading that thing in the Seven Seas'
Review; but you can see that the reviewer swallowed
Geisendanner whole.   He takes your brickyards away
from Nebuchadnezzar and gives them to Nabopolassar,
which seems v-e-r-y c-a-r-e-l-e-s-s!"

This concluding phrase, drawled most Susesquely,
brought a laugh from Burgess, and Pendleton's own
face relaxed.

"They're all flinging Geisendanner at me!" continued Pendleton with renewed animation. "It's hu-
miliating to find the English and Germans alike throwing this impostor at my head. Those fellows began
their excavations secretly and without authority, in a
superstitious belief that they'd find gold images of
heathen gods and all manner of loot there. And it's
hard luck that the confession of one of the conspira-
tors is lost forever and the man himself dead."

"It certainly is most unfortunate!" mourned Mrs.
Burgess, anxious to pour balm upon his wounds.

"It's curious, however, Mr. Pendleton," said Susie
casually, "that I happen to know of the existence of
a copy of that Glosbrenner pamphlet."

"A copy—— You mustn't chaff me about that!"

"Yes," said Susie; "it's really quite the funniest
thing that ever happened."

"This seems to be an important matter, Miss Parker.
You have no right to play upon Mr. Pendleton's cre-
dulity, his hopes!" said Mrs. Burgess icily.

"Nothing like that, Mrs. Burgess!" chirruped Susie.
"I can tell Mr. Pendleton exactly where one copy of
that pamphlet, and probably the only one in the world,
may be found. And a small investment in a night
message to Poughkeepsie will verify what I say. There
is a copy of that pamphlet at Vassar College that was
picked up in Berlin by one of the professors, who gave
it to the library. It had a grayish cover and looked
like a thesis for a doctorate—that sort of thing. It was
a little burned on the edges, and that was one reason
why it caught my eye one day when I was poking
about looking for something among a lot of German
treatises with the most amusing long titles. And it
was a perfectly dee-li-cious story—how they dug and

mixed up those dynasties there; and then one of them wrote a book about it, just for the money he could get out of it. It was all a fake, but they knew enough to make it look like real goods. It was a kind of Huckleberry Finn and Tom Sawyer joke, muddying the water that way."

The conjunction of Huckleberry Finn and Tom Sawyer with Nebuchadnezzar caused even Merrill to laugh.

"I must wire tonight for a confirmation of this—or, perhaps, if you are an alumna of the college you would do it for me."

"I think," said Susie, "they still remember me at college. I was the limit!"

"If what you say is right," Pendleton resumed, "I can smash those Germans and make that Seven Seas' reviewer eat his words! I really believe it would be better for you to wire for me to the librarian for confirmation; I'd rather not publish my anxiety to the world. If you will do this I shall look upon it as the greatest possible favor."

"Delighted!" said Susie, crumpling her napkin.

Mrs. Burgess showed signs of rising, but delayed a moment.

"Miss Parker, you rather implied that there was more than one reason why you happened to notice a singed document in a strange language, bearing upon a subject usually left to scientists and hardly within the range of a young girl's interests. Would you mind enlightening us just a little further in the matter?"

"I thought it was so funny," said Susie, smiling upon them all, "because of my papa."

"Your father?" gasped Mrs. Burgess.

"Yes, Mrs. Burgess. Anything about bricks always seemed to me so amusing, because papa used to own a brickyard."

V

A packet of newspaper clippings forwarded with other mail for Pendleton did not add to the joy of the Burgess breakfast table the next morning. The archæologist murmured an apology and scanned the cuttings with knit brows.

"How early," he asked, "do you imagine Miss Parker can have a confirmation of her impression about that thing of Glosbrenner's?'

"By noon, I should think," answered Burgess.

The husband of Mrs. Burgess had passed a bad night, and he was fully persuaded of the grievousness of his most grievous sin. Never again, he had solemnly sworn, would he attempt any such playfulness as had wrought this catastrophe—never again would he expose himself to the witchery of Susans prone to Susinesses!

"Unless I have corroboration of Miss Parker's impression before three o'clock I shall break my engagement at the state university. With this article in the Seven Seas' Review lying on every college library table, citing Geisendanner against me and discrediting me as the discoverer of the brickyards of Nebuchadnezzar, I shall never stand upon a platform again—and I must withdraw my book. My reputation, in other words, hangs upon a telegram," concluded the archæologist gloomily.

"It is inconceivable," said Mrs. Burgess in a cheerful tone that far from represented her true feelings, "that Miss Parker would have spoken as she did if she hadn't been reasonably confident. Still it is always best to be prepared for disappointments. I think you and Floy had better take the motor for a run into the country and forget the telegram until it arrives. I dare say Miss Parker will send it over at once when it comes."

"Thanks, very much," muttered Pendleton, not highly elated at the thought of motoring with Miss Wilkinson, whose efforts to enliven the breakfast table by talking of things as far removed as possible from the brickyards of oblivion had palled upon the wealthy archæologist. He was an earnest chap, this Pendleton; and the fact that his eligibility as a bachelor was not, in certain eyes, greatly diminished by the failure of his efforts to reëstablish the brick industries of Babylon had not occurred to him. Floy and the Burgesses bored him; but he was dazed by the threatened collapse of his reputation. He declined his host's invitation to walk downtown; and in an equally absent-minded fashion he refused an invitation to luncheon at the University Club, to meet certain prominent citizens. Whereupon, finding the air too tense for his nerves, Burgess left for the bank.

Pendleton moved restlessly about the house, moodily smoking, while the two women pecked at him occasionally with conversation and then withdrew for consultation. His legs seemed to be drawn to those windows of the Burgess drawing room that looked toward the Logans'. In a few minutes Pendleton picked up his hat and stick and left the house, merely saying to the maid he saw clearing up the dining room that he was going for a walk. It is wholly possible he meant to go for a walk quite alone, but at the precise moment at which he reached the Logans' iron gates the Logan door opened suddenly, as though his foot had released a spring, and Susie, in hat and coat, surveyed the world from between the lions. Mrs. Burgess and Floy, established in an upper window, saw Susie wave a hand to Brown Pendleton. For a woman to wave her hand to a man she hasn't known twenty-four hours, particularly when he is wealthy and otherwise distinguished, is the least bit open to criticism. Susie did not escape criticism, but Susie was happily unmindful of it. And it seemed that as she fluttered down between the lions Pendleton grasped her hand anxiously, as though fearing she meditated flight; whereas nothing was further from Susie's mind.

"Good news!" she cried. "They have just telephoned me the answer from the telegraph office. I think telephoned messages are so annoying; and, as they take forever to send one out, I was just going to the office to get it and send it up to you."

"Then," cried Pendleton with fervor, "you must let me go with you. It's a fine morning for a walk."

At the telegraph office he read the message from Susie's friend, the librarian, which was official and final. Whereupon Pendleton became a man of action. To the professor of archæology at Vassar, whom he knew, Pendleton wrote a long message referring to the Seven Seas' Review's attack, and requesting that the precious Glosbrenner confession be carefully guarded until he could examine it personally at the college. He wrote also a cable to the American consul at Berlin, requesting that Geisendanner's whole record be thoroughly investigated.

"Why," asked Susie, an awed witness of this reckless expenditure for telegrams, "why don't you ask the State Department to back up your cable? They must know you in Washington."

"By Jove!" ejaculated Pendleton, staring at Susie as though frightened by her precociousness; "that's a bully idea! Phillips, the second assistant secretary, is an old friend of mine, and he'll tear up the earth for me!"

As they strolled back uptown through the long street, with its arching maples, they seemed altogether like the oldest of friends. Pendleton did not appear to mind at all, if he were conscious of the fact, that Susie's hat was not one of the new fall models, or that her coat was not in the least smart. The strain was over and he submitted himself in high good humor to the Susiness of Susie. It was when they were passing the Public Library that a mood of remorse seized her. There was, she reflected, such a thing as carrying a joke too far. She salved her conscience with the reflection that if she had not yielded to the temptations of her own Susiness and accepted Mr. Burgess' invitation she would not have been able to point this big, earnest student to the particular alcove and shelf where reposed the one copy in all the world of the only document that would rout the critics of the Brickyards of Nebuchadnezzar.

"That Geisendanner," said Susie, rather more soberly than he had yet heard her speak, "was, beyond doubt, an awful liar and a great fraud; but I am a much greater."

"You!" exclaimed Pendleton, leaning for a moment on his stick and staring at her.

"Even so! In the first place, I went to Mrs. Burgess' house for dinner last night through a mistake; she had never seen or heard of me before, and Mr. Burgess asked me merely because he had exhausted the other possibilities and was desperate for some one to fill a chink at his wife's table. And the worst thing I did was to make you think I knew all about Newport, when I was never there in my life—and never saw any of the people I mentioned. Everything I said I got out of the newspapers. It was all just acting, and I put it on a little more because I saw that Mrs. Burgess and her sister didn't like me; they didn't think it was a joke at all, my trying to be Susie again—just once more in my life before I settled back to being called Miss Susan forever. And the way I come to be living in that fine house is simply that I'm borrowed from the library for so much a week to catalogue the Logans' library and push a paperknife through the books. Now you see that Geisendanner isn't in it with me for downright wickedness and most s-h-o-c-k-i-n-g m-e-n-d-a-c-i-t-y!"

"But if you hadn't done all those terrible things where should I be?" demanded Pendleton. "But, before dismissing your confession, would you mind telling me just how you came to know—well, anything about me?"

"I'm almost afraid to go that far," laughed Susie, who, as a matter of fact, did not fear this big, good-natured man at all.

"Tell me that," encouraged Pendleton, "and we will consider the confession closed."

"Well, I think I'll be happier to tell you, and then the slate will be cleaned off a little bit anyhow. A sample copy of the Seven Seas' Review had strayed into the house; and, in glancing over the list of book reviews on the cover, I saw the Brickyards of Nebuchadnezzar among the books noticed. I spent ten minutes reading the review; and then I grabbed the Britannica—four minutes more! And then in Who's Who I saw that you were a Newporter. It's remarkable how educated one can become in fifteen minutes! And, as I said last night when Mrs. Burgess asked me how I came to be interested in that sort of thing, my father ran a brickyard!"

She was looking straight ahead, but the Babylonian

expert saw that there were tears in her eyes, as though called forth by the recollection of other and happier times.

"Thank you," he said gravely; "and now let us forget all about this."

They walked in silence for several minutes, not looking at each other, until she said as they neared the Burgess gate:

"After all, I'm the foolishest little Susie in the world; and it's a lot better for me to go back and be Susan again, and not go to dinner parties where I'm not expected."

And what Pendleton seemed to say, though she was not sure of it, was:

"Never!—not if I know myself!"

.   .   .   .

"Do you suppose," Mrs. Burgess asked her sister as they saw Susie tripping along beside Pendleton, "that she has carried it through?"

"From Brown Pendleton's looks," said Floy, "I should judge she had. But—it can't be possible that she's coming in here again!"

Susie and Pendleton lingered at the gate for an instant, in which he seemed to be talking earnestly. Then together they entered; and in a moment Mrs. Burgess and Floy faced them in the drawing room, where Pendleton announced with undeniable relief and satisfaction the good news from Poughkeepsie.

"Then I suppose you will make the address at the university after all?" said Mrs. Burgess. "I find that so many matters are pressing here that I shall have to forego the pleasure of joining you; and Floy, of course, will have to be excused also."

"On the other hand," said Pendleton with the most

engaging of smiles, "I must beg you not to abandon me. Our party of last night was so perfect, and the results of it so important to me, that I shall greatly regret losing any member of it. I propose in my address tonight to assert my claims to the discovery of the brickyards of Nebuchadnezzar as against all the assertions that contradict me in Geisendanner's romantic fiction about the bronze gates of Babylon. I should like you all to be present, and I am going to beg you, as a particular favor, Mrs. Burgess, to invite Miss Parker to accompany us; for, without her helpful hint as to the existence of that copy of Glosbrenner's confession, where, I should like to know, would I be?"

Mrs. Burgess prided herself upon being able to meet just such situations; and Susie was so demure—there was about the child something so appealing and winning —that Mrs. Burgess dipped her colors.

"Certainly, Mr. Pendleton. I'm sure that Mr. Merrill will feel honored to be included. And I shall be delighted to chaperon Miss Parker."

"Miss Parker has agreed to help me run down some obscure authorities on the mound-builders a little later, and the trip will give her a chance to see what they have in the university library. I can't afford to take any more chances with so much doubtful scientific lore floating about."

"I should think," remarked Floy carelessly, "you would find help of some kind almost essential in your future work."

"I think, myself," said Susie with an uncontrollable resurgence of her Susiness, "that it would save an a-w-f-u-l l-o-t o-f t-r-o-u-b-l-e!"

THE GIRL WITH THE RED FEATHER

I

MR. WEBSTER G. BURGESS, president of the White River National Bank, started slightly as he looked up from the letter he had been reading and found Hill, the Government detective, standing at the rail. Burgess dropped the letter into a drawer and said briskly:

"Hello, Hill—looking for me?"

"No; not yet!"

This was an established form of salutation between them and they both grinned. Burgess rose and leaned against the rail, while the detective summarized his latest counterfeiting adventure, which had to do with a clew furnished by a bad bill that had several weeks earlier got by one of the White River National tellers. Hill had bagged the maker of the bill, and he had just been satisfying himself that the teller would be ready to testify the next day before the Federal grand jury.

Hill visited the bank frequently and Burgess knew him well. The secret-service man was a veteran hunter of offenders against the peace and dignity of the United States, and, moreover, a capital story-teller. Burgess often asked him into his private office for an hour's talk. He had once given a dinner in Hill's honor, inviting a select coterie of friends who knew a good tale when they heard it and appreciated a shrewd, resourceful man when they saw him.

The White River National was one of the largest

and strongest banks in the state, and Burgess was one
of the richest men in his native city of Indianapolis;
but these facts did not interfere with enjoyment of life
according to his lights, which were not unluminous.
Having been born on top, he was not without his
sympathetic interest in the unfortunates whose lot is
cast near the burnt bottom crust, and his generous
impulses sometimes betrayed him into doing things
that carping critics thought not wholly in keeping with
his responsibilities and station in life.

These further facts may be noted: Burgess was the
best-dressed man in Indianapolis—he always wore
a pink carnation; and on occasions when he motored
home for luncheon he changed his necktie—a fact that
did not go unremarked in the bank cages. He belonged
to hunting and fishing clubs in Canada, Maine and
North Carolina, and visited them at proper seasons.
There was a drop of adventurous blood in him that made
banking the least bit onerous at times; and when he
felt the need of air he disappeared to catch salmon or
tarpon, or to hunt grouse or moose. Before his father
had unkindly died and left him the bank and other
profitable embarrassments, he had been obsessed with
a passion for mixing in a South American revolution;
he had chafed when the Spanish War most deplorably
synchronized with the year of his marriage, and he
could think of no valid excuse for leaving the newly
kindled fire on his domestic altar to pose for Spanish
bullets. Twice since his marriage he had looked death
in the eye: once when he tumbled off a crag of the
Canadian Rockies—he was looking for a mountain
sheep; and again when he had been whistled down the
Virginia capes in a hurricane while yachting with a
Boston friend. Every one admitted that he was a

good banker. If he got stung occasionally he did not whimper; and every one knew that the White River National could stand a good deal of stinging without being obliged to hang crape on its front door.

Burgess had always felt that some day something would happen to relieve the monotony of his existence as the chief pilot of an institution which panics always passed by on the other side. His wife cultivated bishops, men of letters and highbrows generally; and he was always stumbling over them in his home, sometimes to his discomfiture. With that perversity of human nature that makes us all pine for what is not, he grew restive under the iron grip of convention and felt that he would like to disappear—either into the wilderness to play at being a savage, or into the shadowy underworld to taste danger and share the experiences of men who fight on the farther side of the barricade.

"You always seem to get 'em, Tom," he remarked to the detective in a familiar tone, bred of long acquaintance. "Just knowing you has made a better man of me. I'm bound to be good as long as you're on the job here; but don't you ever get tired of the game?"

"Well, when you're up against a real proposition and are fencing with a man who's as smart as you are, or smarter, it's some fun; but most of my cases lately have been too tame. The sport isn't what it was when I started. All the crooks are catalogued and photographed and dictagraphed these days; and when you go after 'em you merely send in your card and call a motor to joy-ride 'em to jail. It's been a long time since I was shot at—not since those bill-raisers down in the Orange County hills soaked me with buckshot. When they turn a man loose at Leavenworth we know just about where he will bring up and who's at home to welcome him; and you can usually calculate pretty well just when he will begin manufacturing and floating the queer again."

"You hang on to the petrified idea that once a crook, always a crook—no patience with the eminent thinkers who believe that 'while the lamp holds out to burn, the vilest sinner may return?'"

"Yep—return to jail! Well, I don't say reform is impossible; and I've let a few get by who did keep straight. But it's my business to watch and wait. My best catches have been through luck as much as good management—but don't tell that on me; it would spoil my reputation."

He turned away, glanced across the room and swung round into his former position with his arm resting on the railing by Burgess's desk. He continued talking as before, but the banker saw that something had interested him.

"See that young woman at the paying-teller's cage—halfway down the line—slight, trim, with a red feather in her hat? Take a look."

It was nearing the closing hour and long lines had formed at all the windows. Burgess marked the red feather without difficulty. As the women patrons of the bank were accommodated at a window on the farther side of the lobby he surmised that the young woman was an office clerk on an errand for her employer. She was neatly dressed; there was nothing in her appearance to set her apart from a hundred office girls who visited the bank daily and stood—just as this young woman was standing—in the line of bookkeepers and messengers.

"Well," said the banker, "what about her?"

While looking at the girl the detective drew out a

telegram which he scanned and thrust back into his pocket.

"Her mother runs a boarding house, and her father, Julius Murdock, is a crook—an old yegg—a little crippled by rheumatism now and out of the running. But some of the naughty boys passing this way stop there to rest. The place is—let me see—787 Vevay Street."

Burgess thoughtfully brushed a speck from his coat-sleeve, then looked up indifferently.

"So? Hardly a fashionable neighborhood! Is that what is called a fence?"

"Well, I believe the police did rip up the boarding house a while back, but there was nothing doing. Murdock's able to make a front without visible means of support—may have planted enough stuff to retire on. He's a sort of financial agent and scout for other crooks. They've been in town only a few months. The old man must feel pretty safe or he wouldn't keep his money in a bank. Nellie, out there, is Murdock's daughter, and she's stenographer for the Brooks Lumber Company, over near where they live. When I came in she was at the receiving teller's window with the lumber company's deposit. She's probably waiting to draw a little money now for her daddy. He's one of the few fellows in his line of business who never goes quite broke. Just for fun, suppose you see what he has on the books. If I'm wrong I'll decline that cigar you're going to offer me from the box in your third left-hand drawer." The banker scribbled the name on a piece of paper and sent a boy with it to the head bookkeeper. "And I'd be amused to know how much Nellie is drawing for Julius, too, while you're about it," added the detective, who thereupon sat down in one of the

visitors' chairs inside the railing and became absorbed
in a newspaper.

Burgess strolled across the lobby, stopping to speak
to acquaintances waiting before the several windows—a
common practice of his at the busy hour. Just behind
the girl in the red hat stood a man he knew well; and
he shook hands and continued talking to him, keeping
pace with his friend's progress toward the window.
The girl turned round once and looked at him. He had
a very good view of her face, and she was beyond question a very pretty girl, with strikingly fine gray eyes
and the fresh color of youth. The banker's friend
had been recounting an amusing story and Burgess
was aware that the girl turned her head slightly to
listen; he even caught a gleam of humor in her eyes.
She wore a plain jacket, a year or two out of fashion,
and the red feather in her cloth hat was not so crisp
as it appeared at a distance. She held a check in her
hand ready for presentation; her gloves showed signs of
wear. There was nothing to suggest that she was
other than a respectable young woman, and the
banker resented the detective's implication that she
was the daughter of a crook and lived in a house that
harbored criminals. When she reached the window
Burgess, still talking to the man behind her, heard her
ask for ten-dollar bills.

She took the money and thrust it quickly into a
leathern reticule that swung from her arm. The
banker read the name of the Brooks Lumber Company
on the passbook she held in her hand.

"Pardon me," said Burgess as she stepped away from
the cage——"those are badly worn bills. Let me
exchange them for you."

"Oh, thank you; but it doesn't matter," she said.

Without parleying he stepped to the exchange window, which was free at the moment, and spoke to one of the clerks. The girl opened her reticule and when he turned round she handed him the bills. While the clerk went for the new currency Burgess spoke of the weather and remarked upon the menace of worn bills to public health. They always meant to give women fresh bills, he said; and he wished she would insist upon having them. He was a master of the art of being agreeable, and in his view it was nothing against a woman that she had fine eyes and an engaging smile. Her voice was pleasant to hear and her cheeks dimpled charmingly when she smiled.

"All money looks good to me," she said, thrusting the new bills into her satchel; "but new money is certainly nicer. It always seems like more!"

"But you ought to count that," Burgess protested, not averse to prolonging the conversation. "There's always the possibility of a mistake."

"Well, if there is I'll come back. You'd remember——"

"Oh, yes! I'd remember," replied Burgess with a smile, and then he added hastily: "In a bank it's our business to remember faces!"

"Oh!" said the girl, looking down at her reticule.

Her "oh!" had in it the faintest, the obscurest hint of irony. He wondered whether she resented the idea that he would remember her merely because it was a bank's business to remember faces. Possibly—but no! As she smiled and dimpled he put from him the thought that she wished to give a flirtatious turn to this slight chance interview there in the open lobby of his own bank. Reassured by the smile, supported by the dimples, he said:

"I'm Mr. Burgess; I work here."

"Yes, of course—you're the president. My name is Nellie Murdock."

"You live in Vevay Street?" He dropped his voice. "I can't talk to you here, but I've been asked to see a young man named Drake at your house. Please tell him I'll be there at five-thirty today. You understand?"

"Yes, thank you. He hasn't come yet; but he expected to get in at five." Her lips quivered; she gave him a quick, searching glance, then nodded and walked rapidly out.

Burgess spoke to another customer in the line, with his eyes toward the street, so that he saw the red feather flash past the window and vanish; then he strolled back to where the detective sat. On the banker's desk, face down, lay the memorandum he had sent to the bookkeeper. He turned this up, glanced at it and handed it to Hill.

"Balance $178.18; Julius Murdock," Hill read. "How much did Nellie draw?"

"An even hundred. I stopped to speak to her a moment. Nice girl!"

"Gray eyes, fine teeth, nose slightly snub; laughs easily and shows dimples. Wears usually a gold chain with a gold heart-shaped locket—small diamond in center," said Hill, as though quoting.

"Locket—yes; I did notice the locket," frowned Burgess.

"And you didn't overlook the dimples," remarked the detective—"you can't exactly. By-the-way, you didn't change any money for her yourself?"

"What do you mean?" asked Burgess with a scowl. "Wait!" he added as the detective's meaning dawned upon him.

He went back into the cages. The clerk who had

brought the new bills from the women's department found the old ones where they had been tossed aside by the teller. Burgess carried them to Hill without looking at them. He did not believe what he knew the detective suspected, that the girl was bold enough to try to palm off counterfeit money on a bank—on the president of a bank. He was surprised to find that he was really deeply annoyed by the detective's manner of speaking of Nellie Murdock. He threw the bills down on his desk a little spitefully.

"There you are! That girl took those identical bills out of her satchel and gave them to me to change for new ones. She had plenty of time to slip in a bad bill if she wanted to."

Hill turned round to the light, went over the bills quickly and handed them back to the banker with a grin.

"Good as wheat! I apologize. And I want you to know that I never said she wasn't a pretty girl. And the prettiest ones are often the smartest. It does happen that way sometimes."

"You make me tired, Hill. Everybody you see is crooked. With a man like you there's no such thing as presumption of innocence. 'Way down inside of you you probably think I'm a bit off color too."

"Oh, I wouldn't say just that!" said the detective, laughing and taking the cigar Burgess offered him from a box he produced from his desk. "I must be running along. You don't seem quite as cheerful as usual this morning. I'll come back tomorrow and see if I can't bring in a new story."

Burgess disposed of several people who were waiting to see him, and then took from his drawer the letter he had been reading when the detective interrupted him. It was from Ralph Gordon, a Chicago lawyer, who was widely known as an authority on penology. Burgess had several times contributed to the funds of a society of which Gordon was president, whose function it was to meet criminals on their discharge from prison and give them a helping hand upward.

The banker had been somewhat irritated today by Hill's manner of speaking of the criminals against whom he was pitted; and doubtless Hill's attitude toward the young woman he had pointed out as the daughter of a crook added to the sympathetic feeling with which Burgess took up his friend's letter for another reading. The letter ran:

Dear Old Man: You said last fall that you wished I'd put you in the way of knowing one of the poor fellows I constantly meet in the work of our society. I'm just now a good deal interested in a young fellow—Robert Drake by name—whose plight appeals to me particularly. He is the black sheep of a fine family I know slightly in New England. Drink was his undoing, and after an ugly scrape in college he went down fast—*facilis descensus*; the familiar story. The doors at home were closed to him, and after a year or two he fell in with one of the worst gangs of yeggs in the country. He was sent up for cracking a safe in a Southern Illinois post-office. The agent of our society at Leavenworth has had an eye on him; when he was discharged he came straight to me and I took him into my house until we could plan something for him. I appealed to his family and they've sent me money for his use. He wants to go to the Argentine Republic—thinks he can make a clean start down there. But there are difficulties. Unfortunately there's just now an epidemic of yegging in the Middle West and all suspects are being gathered in. Of course Drake isn't safe, having just done time for a similar offense. I've arranged with Saxby— Big Billy, the football half-back—you remember him—to ship Drake south on one of the Southern Cross steamers. Saxby is, as you know, manager of the company at New Orleans. I wanted to send Drake down direct— but here's the rub: there's a girl in Indianapolis he wants to marry and take along with him. He got acquainted with her in the underworld, and her people, he confesses, are a shady lot. He insists that she is straight, and it's for her he wants to take a fresh grip and begin over again. So tomorrow—that's January twenty-third—he will be at her house in your city, 787 Vevay Street; and he means to marry her. It's better for him not to look you up; and will you, as the good fellow you are, go to see him and give him cash for the draft for five hundred dollars I'm inclosing? Another five hundred—all this from his father —I'm sending to Saxby to give him in gold aboard the steamer. Drake believes that in a new country, with the girl to help him, he can make good.

Hoping this isn't taking advantage of an old and valued friendship, I am always, dear old man—

Burgess put the letter in his pocket, signed his mail, entertained in the directors' room a committee of the Civic League, subscribed a thousand dollars to a hospital, said yes or no to a number of propositions, and then his wife called him on the telephone, with an intimation that their regular dinner hour was seven.

She reminded him of this almost daily, as Burgess sometimes forgot to tell her when he was to dine downtown.

"Anybody for dinner tonight?"

"Yes, Web," she answered in the meek tone she reserved for such moments as this. "Do I have to tell you again that this is the day Bishop Gladding is to be here? He said not to try to meet him, as he didn't know what train he'd take from Louisville, but he'd show up in time for dinner. He wrote he was coming a week ago, and you said not to ask anybody for dinner, as you liked to have him to yourself. You don't mean to tell me——"

"No, Gertie; I'll be there!" and then, remembering that his too-ready acquiescence might establish a precedent that would rise up and smite him later, he added: "But these are busy days; if I should be late don't wait for me. That's the rule, you know."

"I should think, Web, when the bishop is an old friend, and saved your life that time you and Ralph Gordon were hunting Rocky Mountain sheep with him, and the bishop nearly died carrying you back to a doctor—I should think——"

"Oh, I'll be there," said Burgess; "but there's a friend of Gordon's in town I'll have to look up after a little. No; he hasn't time to come to the house. You know how it is, Gertie——"

She said she knew how it was. These telephonic colloquies were not infrequent between the Burgesses, and Mrs. Burgess was not without her provocation. He resolved to hurry and get through with Gordon's man, Drake, the newly freed convict seeking a better life, that he might not be late to dinner in his own house, which was to be enlivened by the presence of the young, vigorous missionary bishop, who was, moreover, a sportsman and in every sense a man's man.

He put on his ulster, made sure of the five hundred dollars he had obtained on Gordon's draft, and at five-thirty went out to his car, which had waited an hour.

II

A thaw had been in progress during the day and hints of rain were in the air. The moon tottered drunkenly among flying clouds. The bank watchman predicted snow before morning as he bade Burgess good night.

Burgess knew Vevay Street, for he owned a business block at its intersection with Senate Avenue. Beyond the avenue it deteriorated rapidly and was filled with tenements and cheap boarding houses. Several blocks west ran an old canal, lined with factories, elevators, lumber yards and the like, and on the nearer bank was a network of railroad switches.

He thought it best not to approach the Murdock house in his motor; so he left it at the drug-store corner, and, bidding the chauffeur wait for him, walked down Vevay Street looking for 787. It was a forbidding thoroughfare and the banker resolved to complain to the Civic League; it was an outrage that such Stygian blackness should exist in a civilized city, and he meant to do something about it. When he found the number it proved to be half of a ramshackle two-story double house. The other half was vacant and plastered with For Rent signs. He struck a match and read a dingy card that announced rooms and boarding. The window shades were pulled halfway down, showing lights in the front room. Burgess knocked and in a moment the door was opened guardedly by a stocky, bearded man.

"Mr. Murdock?"

"Well, what do you want?" growled the man, widening the opening a trifle to allow the hall light behind him to fall on the visitor's face.

"Don't be alarmed. A friend of Robert Drake's in Chicago asked me to see him. My errand is friendly."

A woman's voice called from the rear of the hall:

"It's all right, dad; let the gentleman in."

Murdock slipped the bolt in the door and then scrutinized Burgess carefully with a pair of small, keen eyes. As he bent over the lock the banker noted his burly frame and the powerful arms below his rolled-up shirtsleeves.

"Just wait there," he said, pointing to the front room. He closed the hall door and Burgess heard his step on the stairs.

An odor of stale cooking offended the banker's sensitive nostrils. The furniture was the kind he saw daily in the windows of furniture stores that sell on the installment plan; on one side was an upright piano, with its top littered with music. Now that he was in the house, he wondered whether this Murdock was after all a crook, and whether the girl with the red feather, with her candid eyes, could possibly be his daughter. His wrath against Hill rose again as he recalled his cynical tone—and on the thought the girl appeared from a door at the farther end of the room.

She bade him "Good evening!" and they shook hands. She had just come from her day's work at the lumber company's office, she explained. He found no reason for reversing his earlier judgment that she was a very

pretty girl. Now that her head was free of the hat
with the red feather, he saw that her hair, caught up in
a becoming pompadour, was brown, with a golden
glint in it. Her gray eyes seemed larger in the light of
the single gas-burner than they had appeared by daylight at the bank. There was something poetic and
dreamy about them. Her age he placed at about half his
own, but there was the wisdom of the centuries in
those gray eyes of hers. He felt young before her.

"There was a detective in the bank when I was in
there this morning. He knew me," she said at once.

"Yes; he spoke of you," said Burgess.

"And he knows—what does he know?"

The girl's manner was direct; he felt that she was
entitled to a frank response.

"He told me your father had been—we will say
suspected in times past; that he had only lately come
here; but, unless he deceived me, I think he has no
interest in him just now. The detective is a friend
of mine. He visits the bank frequently. It was just
by chance that he spoke of you."

"You didn't tell him that Mr. Gordon had asked you
to come here?"

"No; Drake wasn't mentioned."

Nellie nodded; she seemed to be thinking deeply.
Her prettiness was enhanced, he reflected, by the few
freckles that clustered about her nose. And he was
ready to defend the nose which the detective, reciting
from his card catalogue, had called snub!

"Did your friend tell you Bob wants to be married
before he leaves? I suppose you don't know that?"

She blushed, confirming his suspicion that it was she
whom Drake was risking arrest to marry.

"Yes; and if I guess rightly that you're the girl I'd like to say that he's an extremely fortunate young man! You don't mind my saying that!"

He wondered whether all girls who have dimples blush to attract attention to them. The point interested Webster G. Burgess. The thought that Nellie Murdock meant to marry a freshly discharged convict, no matter how promising he might be, was distasteful to him; and yet her loyalty and devotion increased his admiration. There was romance here, and much money had not hardened the heart of Webster G. Burgess.

"It all seems too good to be true," she said happily, "that Bob and I can be married after all and go away into a new world where nobody knows us and he can start all over again." And then, coloring prettily: "We're all ready to go except getting married—and maybe you can help us find a minister."

"Easily! But I'm detaining you. Better have Drake come in; I want to speak to him, and then we can make all the arrangements in a minute."

"I'm afraid he's been watched; it's brutal for them to do that when he's done his time and means to live straight! I wonder——" She paused and the indignation that had flashed out in her speech passed quickly. "It's asking a great deal, Mr. Burgess, but would you let us leave the house with you? The quicker we go the better—and a man of your position wouldn't be stopped. But if you'd rather not——"

"I was just going to propose that! Please believe that in every way I am at your service."

His spirits were high. It would give edge to the encounter to lend his own respectability to the flight.

The idea of chaperoning Nellie Murdock and her convict lover through an imaginable police picket pleased him.

She went out and closed the door. Voices sounded in the hall; several people were talking earnestly. When the door opened a man dodged quickly into the room, the girl following.

"This is Robert Drake, Mr. Burgess. Bob, this is the gentleman Mr. Gordon told you about."

Burgess experienced a distinct shock of repulsion as the man shuffled across the room to shake hands. A stubble of dark beard covered his face, his black hair was crumpled, and a long bang of it lying across his forehead seemed to point to his small, shifty blue eyes. His manner was anxious; he appeared decidedly ill at ease. Webster G. Burgess was fastidious and this fellow's gray suit was soiled and crumpled, and he kept fingering his collar and turning it up round a very dirty neck.

"Thank you, sir—thank you!" he repeated nervously.

A door slammed upstairs and the prospective bridegroom started perceptibly and glanced round. But Burgess's philosophy rallied to his support. This was the fate of things, one of life's grim ironies—that a girl like Nellie Murdock, born and reared in the underworld, should be linking herself to an outlaw. After all, it was not his affair. Pretty girls in his own world persisted in preposterous marriages. And Bob grinned cheerfully. Very likely with a shave and a bath and a new suit of clothes he would be quite presentable. The banker had begun to speak of the route to be taken to New Orleans when a variety of things happened so quickly that Burgess's wits were put to high tension to keep pace with them.

The door by the piano opened softly. A voice recognizable as that of Murdock spoke sharply in a low tone:

"Nellie, hit up the piano! Stranger, walk to the window—slow—and yank the shade! Bob, cut up-stairs!"

These orders, given in the tone of one used to command, were quickly obeyed. It was in the banker's mind the moment he drew down the shade that by some singular transition he, Webster G. Burgess, had committed himself to the fortunes of this dubious household. If he walked out of the front door it would likely be into the arms of a policeman; and the fact of a man of his prominence being intercepted in flight from a house about to be raided would not look well in the newspapers. Nellie, at the piano, was playing Schubert's Serenade—and playing it, he thought, very well. The situation was not without its humor; and here, at last, was his chance to see an adventure through. He heard Bob take the stairs in three catlike jumps. Nellie, at the piano, said over her shoulder, with Schubert's melody in her eyes:

"This isn't funny; but they wouldn't dare touch you! You'd better camp right here."

"Not if I know myself!" said Burgess with decision as he buttoned his ulster.

She seemed to accept his decision as a matter of course and, still playing, indicated the door, still ajar, through which the disconcerting orders had been spoken. Burgess stepped into a room where a table was partly set for supper.

"This ain't no place for you, stranger!" said Murdock harshly. "How you goin' to get away?"

"I'll follow Bob. If he makes it I can."

"Humph! This party's too big now. You ought to have kept out o' this."

There was a knock at the front door and Murdock pointed an accusing finger at Burgess.

"Either set down and play it out or skip!" He jerked his head toward the stairs. The music ceased at the knock. "Nellie, what's the answer?"

Murdock apparently deferred to Nellie in the crisis; and as the knock was repeated she said:

"I'll get Bob and this gentleman out. Don't try to hold the door—let 'em in."

Before he knew what was happening, Burgess was at the top of the stairway, with the girl close at his heels. She opened a door into a dark room.

"Bob!" she called.

"All right!" whispered Drake huskily.

Near the floor Burgess marked Bob's position by a match the man struck noiselessly, shielding it in the curve of his hand at arm's length. It was visible for a second only. Nellie darted lightly here and there in the dark. A drawer closed softly; Burgess heard the swish of her jacket as she snatched it up and drew it on. The girl undoubtedly knew what she was about. Then a slim, cold hand clutched his in a reassuring clasp. Another person had entered the room and the doorkey clicked.

"Goodby, mother!" Burgess heard the girl whisper.

The atmosphere changed as the steps of the three refugees echoed hollowly in an empty room. A door closed behind them and there was a low rumble as a piece of furniture was rolled against it. Burgess was amazed to find how alert all his senses were. He

heard below the faint booming of voices as Murdock
entertained the police.   In the pitch-dark he found
himself visualizing the room into which they had passed
and the back stairway down which they crept to the
kitchen of the vacant half of the house.   As they paused
there to listen something passed between Drake and
Nellie.

"Give it to me—quick!   I gotta shake that guy!"
Drake whispered hoarsely.

The girl answered:

"Take it, but keep still and I'll get you out o' this."

Burgess thought he had struck at her; but she made
no sign.   She took the lead and opened the kitchen
door into a shed; then the air freshened and he felt
rain on his face.   They stood still for an instant.
Some one, apparently at the Murdock kitchen door,
beat three times on a tin pan.

"There are three of them!" whispered Nellie.
"One's likely to be at the back gate.   Take the side
fence!"   She was quickly over; and then began a rapid
leaping of the partition fences of the narrow lots of the
neighborhood.   At one point Burgess's ulster ripped on a
nail; at another place he dropped upon a chicken coop,
where a lone hen squawked her terror and indignation.
It had been some time since Webster G. Burgess had
jumped fences, and he was blowing hard when finally they
reached a narrow alley.   He hoped the hurdling was at
an end, but a higher barricade confronted them than
the low fences they had already negotiated.   Nellie
and Bob whispered together a moment; then Bob
took the fence quickly and silently.   Burgess jumped
for the top, but failed to catch hold.   A second try
was luckier, but his feet thumped the fence furiously
as he tried to mount.

"Cheese it on the drum!" said Nellie, and she gave his

legs a push that flung him over and he tumbled into
the void. "Bob mustn't bolt; he always goes crazy and
wants to shoot the cops," he heard her saying, so close
that he felt her breath on his cheek. "I had to give
him that hundred——"

A man ran through the alley they had just left.
From the direction of Vevay Street came disturbing
sounds as the Murdocks' neighbors left their supper
tables for livelier entertainment outside.

"If it's cops they'll make a mess of it—I was afraid
it was Hill," said the girl.

It already seemed a good deal of a mess to Burgess.
He had got his bearings and knew they were in the huge
yard of the Brooks Lumber Company. Great piles of
lumber deepened the gloom. The scent of new pine
was in the moist air. Nellie was already leading the
way down one of the long alleys between the lumber.
A hinge creaked stridently behind them. The three
stopped, huddled close together. The opaque darkness
seemed now to be diminishing slightly as the moon and
a few frightened stars shone out of the clouds. Then
the blackness was complete again.

"They've struck the yard!" said Nellie. "That was
the Wood Street gate."

"If they stop to open gates they're not much good,"
said the banker largely, in the tone of one who does
not pause for gates.

The buttons had been snapped from his ulster at
the second fence and this garment now hung loosely
round him, a serious impediment to flight. He made
a mental note to avoid ulsters in future. A nail had
scraped his shin, and when he stopped to rub it he
discovered an ugly rent in his trousers. Nellie kept
moving. She seemed to know the ways of the yard

and threaded the black lumber alleys with ease. They were close together, running rapidly, when she paused suddenly. Just ahead of them in a cross alley a lantern flashed. It was the lumber company's private watchman. He stopped uncertainly, swung his lantern into the lane where the trio waited, and hurried on.

They were halfway across the yard as near as Burgess could judge, hugging the lumber piles closely and stopping frequently to listen, when they were arrested by a sound behind. The moon had again swung free of clouds and its light flooded the yard. The distance of half a block behind a policeman stood in the alley they had just traversed. He loomed like a heroic statue in his uniform overcoat and helmet. His shout rang through the yard.

"Beat it!" cried Nellie.

III

Nellie was off as she gave the word. They struck a well-beaten cross-alley—a main thoroughfare of the yard—and sprinted off at a lively gait. It was in Burgess's mind that it was of prime importance that Drake should escape—it was to aid the former convict that he had involved himself in this predicament; and even if the wedding had to be abandoned and the girl left behind it was better than for them all to be caught. He was keeping as close as possible to Bob, but the young man ran with incredible swiftness; and he now dodged into one of the narrower paths and vanished.

The yard seemed more intricate than ever with its network of paths, along which the lumber stacks rose fantastically. Looking over his shoulder, Burgess saw that the single policeman had been reenforced by

another man. It was a real pursuit now—there was no
belittling that fact. A revolver barked and a fusillade
followed. Then the moon was obscured and the
yard was black again. Burgess felt himself jammed in
between two tall lumber piles.

"Climb! Get on top quick and lie down!"

Nellie was already mounting; he felt for the strips
that are thrust between planks to keep them from
rotting, grasped them and gained the top. It was a
solid pile and it lifted him twenty feet above the ground.
He threw himself flat just as the pursuers rushed by;
and when they were gone he sat up and nursed his
knees. He marked Nellie's position by her low laugh.
He was glad she laughed. He was glad she was there!

Fifty yards away a light flashed—a policeman had
climbed upon a tall pile of lumber and was whipping
about him with a dark lantern.

"It will take them all night to cover this yard that
way," she whispered, edging close. "They're crossing the yard the way women do when they're trying
to drive chickens into a coop. They won't find Bob
unless they commit burglary."

"How's that?" asked Burgess, finding a broken cigar
in his waistcoat pocket and chewing the end.

"Oh, I gave him the key to the office and told him to
sit on the safe. It's a cinch they won't look for him
there; and we've got all night to get him out."

Burgess was flattered by the plural. Her good
humor was not without its effect on him. The
daughter of the retired yeggman was a new kind of girl,
and one he was glad to add to his collection of feminine
types. He wished she would laugh oftener.

The president of the White River National Bank,
perched on a pile of lumber on a wet January evening

with a girl he knew only as his accomplice in an escapade that it would be very difficult to explain to a cynical world, reflected that at about this hour his wife, hardly a mile distant, in one of the handsomest houses in town, was dressing for dinner to be ready to greet a guest, who was the most valiant member of the sedate House of Bishops.   And Webster G. Burgess assured himself that he was not a bit frightened; he had been pursued by detectives and police and shot at—and yet he was less annoyed than when the White River National lost an account, or an ignorant new member preempted his favorite seat in the University Club dining room.   He had lost both the sense of fear and the sense of shame; and he marveled at his transformation and delighted in it.

"How long will it be before that begins to bore them, Nellie?" he remarked casually, as though he were speaking to a girl he had known always, in a cozy corner at a tea.

The answer was unexpected and it did not come from Nellie.   He heard the scraping of feet, and immediately a man loomed against the sky not thirty feet away and began sweeping the neighboring stacks with an electric lamp; its rays struck Burgess smartly across the face. He hung and jumped; and as he let go the light flashed again and an automatic barked.

"Lord!   It's Hill!" he gasped.

As he struck the ground he experienced a curious tingle on the left side of his head above the ear—it was as though a hot needle had been drawn across it.   The detective yelled and fired another shot to attract the attention of the other pursuers.   Nellie was already down and ready for flight.   She grasped Burgess' arm and hurried him over and between unseen obstacles. There seemed to be no method of locomotion to which he was not urged—climbing, crawling, running, edging in between seeming Gibraltars of lumber. From a low pile she leaped to a higher, and on up until they were thirty feet above the ground; then it seemed to amuse her to jump from pile to pile until they reached earth again. Running over uneven lumber piles in the dark, handicapped by an absurd ulster, does not make for ease, grace or security—and wet lumber has a disagreeable habit of being slippery.

They trotted across an open space and crept under a shingle shed.

"Good place to rest," panted Nellie—and he dropped down beside her on a bundle of shingles. The rain fell monotonously upon the low roof of their shelter.

"That's a pretty picture," said the girl dreamily.

Burgess, breathing like a husky bellows, marveled at her. What had interested her was the flashing of electric lamps from the tops of the lumber piles, where the pursuers had formed a semicircle and were closing in on the spot where the quarry had disappeared. They were leaping from stack to stack, shooting their lamps ahead.

"The lights dancing round that way are certainly picturesque," observed Burgess. "Whistler would have done a charming nocturne of this. I doubt whether those fellows know what a charm they impart to the mystical, moist night. The moving pictures ought to have this. What's our next move?" he asked, mopping his wet face with his handkerchief.

"I've got to get Bob out of the office and then take a long jump. And right here's a good time for you to skedaddle. You can drop into the alley back of this shed and walk home."

"Thanks—but nothing like that! I've got to see you married and safely off. I'd never dare look Gordon in the face if I didn't."

"I thought you were like that," she said gently, and his heart bounded at her praise. She stole away into the shadows, and he stared off at the dancing lights where the police continued their search.

Far away the banker saw the aura of the city, and he experienced again a sensation of protest and rebellion. He wondered whether this was the feeling of the hunted man—the man who is tracked and driven and shot at! He, Webster G. Burgess, had been the target of a bullet; and, contrary to every rule of the life in which he had been reared, he was elated to have been the mark for a detective's gun. He knew that he should feel humiliated—that he owed it to himself, to his wife waiting for him at home, to his friends, to society itself, to walk out and free himself of the odium that would attach to a man of his standing who had run with the hare when his place by all the canons was with the hounds. And then, too, this low-browed criminal was not the man for a girl like Nellie to marry —he could not free himself of that feeling.

As he pondered this she stole back to his hiding-place. The ease, lightness and deftness with which she moved amazed him; he had not known she was near until he heard Drake's heavier step beside her.

"Bob's here, all right. We must march again," she said.

She explained her plan and the three started off briskly, reached a fence—the world seemed to be a tangle of fences!—and dropped over into a coalyard. Burgess was well muddled again, but Nellie never hesitated. It had grown colder; heavier clouds had drifted across the heavens and snow began to fall. They reached the farther bound of the coalyard safely; and as they were about to climb out a dog yelped and rushed at them.

"I forgot about that dog! Over, quick! The watchman for this yard is probably back there playing with the police, or else he's hiding himself," said Nellie.

This proved to be the most formidable fence of the series for Burgess, and his companions got him over with difficulty just as a dog snapped at his legs. They landed in a tangle of ice-covered weeds and lay still a moment. Bob was in bad humor, and kept muttering and cursing.

"Chuck it, Bob!" said Nellie sharply.

They were soon jumping across the railroad switches and could see the canal stretching toward the city, marked by a succession of well-lighted bridges.

"They'll pinch us here! Nellie, you little fool, if you hadn't steered me to that office I'd 'a' been out o' this!"

He swore under his breath and Burgess cordially hated him for swearing at the girl. But, beyond doubt, the pursuers had caught the scent and were crossing the coalyard. They heard plainly the sounds of men running and shouting. Bob seized Nellie and there was a sharp tussle.

"For God's sake, trust me, Bob! Take this; don't let him have it!" And she thrust a revolver into Burgess's hand. "Better be caught than that! Mind the bank here and keep close together. Good dog—he's eating the cops!" And she laughed her delicious mirthful laugh. A pistol banged and the dog barked no more.

The three were now on the ice of the canal, spreading out to distribute their weight. The day had been warm enough to soften the ice and it cracked ominously as the trio sped along. Half a dozen bridges were plainly in sight toward the city and Burgess got his bearings again. Four blocks away was his motor and the big car was worth making a break for at any hazard. They stopped under the second bridge and heard the enemy charging over the tracks and out upon the ice. A patrol wagon clanged on a bridge beyond the coalyard and a whistle blew.

A sergeant began bawling orders and half a dozen men were sent to reconnoiter the canal. As they advanced they swept the banks with their electric lamps and conferred with scouts flung along the banks. The snow fell steadily.

"We can't hold this much longer," said Nellie; and as she spoke there was a wild shout from the party advancing over the ice. The lamps of several policemen shot wildly into the sky and there were lusty bawls for help.

"A bunch of fat cops breaking through the ice!" chuckled the girl, hurrying on.

They gained a third bridge safely, Nellie frequently admonishing Bob to stick close to her. It was clear enough to Burgess that Drake wanted to be rid of him and the girl and take charge of his own destiny. Burgess had fallen behind and was feeling his way under the low bridge; Nellie was ahead, and the two men were for the moment flung together.

"Gi' me my gun! I ain't goin' to be pinched this trip. Gi' me the gun!"

"Keep quiet; we're all in the same boat!" panted Burgess, whose one hundred and seventy pounds, as

registered on the club scales that very day after luncheon, had warned him that he was growing pulpy.

The rails on the bank began to hum, and a switch
engine, picking up cars in the neighboring yards,
puffed along the bank. Burgess felt himself caught
suddenly round the neck and before he knew what
was happening landed violently on his back. He
struggled to free himself, but Bob gripped his throat
with one hand and snatched the revolver from his
pocket with the other. It was all over in a minute.
The rattle of the train drowned the sound of the
attack, and when Nellie ran back to urge them on
Burgess was just getting on his feet and Bob had
vanished.

"I couldn't stop him—he grabbed the gun and ran,"
Burgess explained. "He must have jumped on that
train."

"Poor Bob!" She sighed deeply; a sob broke from
her. Her arms went around Burgess's neck. "Poor
Bob! Poor old Bob!"

The locomotive bell clanged remotely. It was very
still, and Mr. Webster G. Burgess, president of the
White River National Bank, stood there under a canal
bridge with the arms of a sobbing girl round his neck!
Under all the circumstances it was wholly indefensible,
and the absurdity of it was not lost upon him. Drake
had bolted, and all this scramble with the ex-convict
and his sweetheart had come to naught.

"He'll get away; he was desperate and he didn't
trust me. He didn't even wait for the money Gordon
sent me!"

"Oh!"—she faltered, and her breath was warm on
his cheek—"that wasn't Drake!"

"It wasn't Robert Drake?" Burgess blurted. "Not Drake?"

"No; it was Bob, my stepbrother. He got into trouble in Kentucky and came here to hide, and I was trying to help him; and I'll miss Robert—and you've spoiled your clothes—and they shot at you!"

"It was poor shooting," said Burgess critically as the red feather brushed his nose; "but we've got to clear out of this or we'll be in the patrol wagon in a minute!"

It was his turn now to take the initiative. His first serious duty was to become a decent, law-abiding citizen again, and he meant to effect the transformation as quickly as possible. He began discreetly by unclasping the girl's arms.

"Stop crying, Nellie—you did the best you could for Bob; and now we'll get out of this and tackle Drake's case. When that wagon that's coming has crossed this bridge we'll stroll over to Senate Avenue, where my car's waiting, and beat it."

IV

The policemen had been pried out of the ice and the search continued, though the spirit seemed to have gone out of it. The scouting party had scattered among the grim factories along the railway tracks. Bob had presumably been borne out of the zone of danger and there was nothing more to be done for him.

They waited to make sure they were not watched and then crawled up the bank into Vevay Street. The rapidly falling snow enfolded them protectingly. Now that life had grown more tranquil Burgess became

conscious that the scratch above his left ear had not
ceased tingling.   It was with real emotion that Webster
G. Burgess reflected that he had escaped death by a
hairbreadth.   He meant to analyze that emotion later
at his leisure.   The grazing of his head by that bullet
marked the high moment of his life; the memory of it
would forever be the chief asset among all his experiences.   There was a wet line down his cheek to
his shirt collar that he had supposed to be perspiration;
but his handerchief now told another story.   He
turned up the collar of his buttonless ulster to hide
any tell-tale marks of his sins and knocked his battered
cap into shape.   Glancing down at Nellie, he saw that
the red feather had not lost its jauntiness, and she
tripped along placidly, as though nothing unusual had
happened; but as they passed opposite the Murdock
house, where a lone policeman patrolled the walk, her
hand tightened on his arm and he heard her saying, as
though to herself:

"Goodby, house!   Goodby, dad and mother!   I'll
never be back any more."

Burgess quickly shut the door of the tonneau upon
Nellie; he had cranked the machine and was drawing on
the chauffeur's gauntlets, which he had found in the
driver's seat, when the druggist ran out and accosted
him.

"Hello, Miller!   Seen anything of my chauffeur?"

"I guess he's out with the police," the man answered
excitedly; "they've been chasing a bunch o' crooks over
there somewhere.   Two or three people have been shot.
There was a woman mixed up in the scrimmage, but
she got away."

"Yes; it was a big fight—a whole gang of toughs!
I took a short dash with the police myself, and fell

over a dead man and scratched my ear. No, thanks; I'll fix it up later. By-the-way, when my man turns up you might tell him to come home—if that harmonizes with his own convenience." He stepped into the car. "Oh, has the plumber fixed that drain for you yet? Well, the agent ought to look after such things. Call me up in a day or two if he doesn't attend to it."

It was rather cheering, on the whole, to be in the open again, and he lingered, relishing his freedom, his immunity from molestation. The very brick building before which he stood gave him a sense of security; he was a reputable citizen and property owner—not to be trifled with by detectives and policemen. A newspaper reporter whom he knew jumped from a passing street car, recognized him and asked excitedly where the bodies had been taken.

"They're stacked up like cordwood," answered Burgess, "over in the-lumber-yard. Some of the cops went crazy and are swimming in the canal. Young lady—guest of my wife—and I came over to look after sick family, and ran into the show. I joined the hunt for a while, but it wasn't any good. You'll find the survivors camped along the canal bank waiting for reenforcements."

He lighted a cigarette, jumped in and drove the car toward home for half a dozen blocks—then lowered the speed so that he could speak to the girl. He was half sorry the adventure was over; but there yet remained his obligation to do what he could for Drake—if that person could be found.

"You must let me go now," said Nellie earnestly; "the police will wake up and begin looking for me, and you've had trouble enough. And it was rotten for me to work you to help get Bob off! You'd better have stayed in the house; but I knew you would help—and I was afraid Bob would kill somebody. Please let me out right here!"

Her hand was on the latch.

"Oh, never in this world! I have no intention of letting the police take you—you haven't done anything but try to help your brother, like the fine girl you are; and that's all over. Where's Drake?"

Her gravity passed instantly and her laugh greeted his ears again. He was running the car slowly along a curb, his head bent to hear.

"Listen! Robert telephoned just as I was leaving the office. I told him to keep away from the house. When I saw you in the bank I knew Bob was here, but I thought he'd be out of the way; but he wouldn't go until dark, and I would have telephoned you but I was afraid. I really meant to tell you at the house that Robert wasn't there and wouldn't be there; but Bob was so ugly I made you go with us, because I wanted your help. I thought if they nailed us you would pull Bob through. And now you don't really mind—do you?" she concluded tearfully.

"Well, what about Drake? If he's still——"

She bent closer and he heard her murmurous laugh again.

"I told Robert I'd meet him at the courthouse—by the steps nearest the police station—at seven o'clock. That's the safest place I could think of."

Burgess nodded and the machine leaped forward.

"We've got ten minutes to keep that date, Nellie. But I'm going to be mighty late for dinner!"

V

As Nellie jumped from the car at the courthouse a young man stepped out of the shadows instantly. Only a few words passed between them. Burgess opened the door for them and touched his hat as he snapped on the electric bulb in the tonneau. Glancing round when he had started the car, Burgess saw that Drake had clasped Nellie's hand; and there was a resolute light in the young man's eyes—his face had the convict's pallor, but he looked sound and vigorous. On the whole, Robert Drake fulfilled the expectations roused by Gordon's letter—he was neatly dressed, and his voice and manner bespoke the gentleman. One or two questions put by the banker he answered reassuringly. He had reached the city at five o'clock and had not been interfered with in any way.

As they rolled down Washington Street a patrol passed them, moving slowly toward the police station. Burgess fancied there was dejection in the deliberate course of the wagon homeward, and he grinned to himself; but when he looked around Nellie's face was turned away from the street toward the courthouse clock, to which she had drawn Drake's attention as the wagon passed.

"Are you and Nellie going to be married? That's the first question."

"Yes, sir; it's all on the square. There's a lawyer here who got me out of a scrape once and he helped me get the license. If you'll take us to a minister—that's all we want."

"Oh, the minister will be easy!"

"Now," he said as they reached his home, "come along with me and do exactly what I tell you. And don't be scared!"

The evening had been full of surprises, but he meant now to cap the series of climaxes, that had mounted so rapidly, with another that should give perfect symmetry to the greatest day of his life. They entered the house through a basement door and gained the second floor by the back stairs. Nora, his wife's maid, came from one of the rooms and he gave her some orders.

"This is Miss Murdock. She's just come in from a long journey and I wish you would help her touch up a bit. Go into Mrs. Burgess's room and get anything you need. Miss Murdock has lost her bag, and has to be off again in half an hour; so fix up a suitcase for her—you'll know how. It will be all right with Mrs. Burgess. How far's the dinner got? Just had salad? All right. Come with me, Drake."

In his own dressing room he measured the young man with his eye. Mindful of Gordon's injunction that Drake might be picked up by the police, he went into the guest room, tumbled over the effects of the Bishop of Shoshone and threw out a worn sackcoat, a clerical waistcoat and trousers, and handed them to his guest.

Webster G. Burgess prided himself on being able to dress in ten minutes; in fifteen on this occasion he not only refreshed himself with a shower but tended his bruises and fitted a strip of invisible plaster to the bullet scratch above his ear. His doffed business suit and ulster he flung into the laundry basket in the bathroom; then he went into the guest room to speak to Drake.

"It was bully of you to stand by Nellie in her trouble!"

said Drake with feeling. "I guess you came near getting pinched."

"Oh, it was nothing," remarked Burgess, shooting his cuffs with the air of a gentleman to whom a brush with the police is only part of the day's work.

"Nellie told me about it, coming up in the machine. I guess you're a good sport, all right."

Webster G. Burgess was conscious of the ex-convict's admiration; he was not only aware that Drake regarded him admiringly but he found that he was gratified by the approbation of this man who had cracked safes and served time for it.

"Nellie is a great girl!" said Burgess, to change the subject. "I believe you mean to be good to her. You're a mighty lucky boy to have a girl like that ready to stand by you! Here's some money Gordon asked me to give you. And here's something for Nellie, a check—one thousand—Saxby will cash it for you at New Orleans. Please tell your wife to-morrow that it's my wife's little wedding gift, in token of Nellie's kindness in keeping me out of jail. Now where's that marriage license? Good! There's a bishop in this house who will marry you; we'll go down and pull it off in a jiffy. Then you can have a nibble of supper and we'll take you to the station. There's a train for the South at eight-twenty."

Nellie was waiting in the hall when they went out. Nora had dressed her hair, and bestowed upon her a clean collar and a pair of white gloves. She had exchanged her shabby, wet tan shoes for a new pair Mrs. Burgess had imported from New York. The mud acquired in the scramble through the lumber-yard had been carefully scraped from her skirt. Voices were heard below.

"They've just come in from dinner," said the maid, "Shall I tell Bridget to keep something for you?"

"Yes—something for three, to be on the table in fifteen minutes."

Mrs. Webster G. Burgess always maintains that nothing her husband may do can shock her. When her husband had not appeared at seven she explained to her guest that he had been detained by an unexpected meeting of a clearing-house committee, it being no harder to lie to a bishop than to any one else when a long-suffering woman is driven to it. She was discussing with the Bishop of Shoshone the outrageously feeble support of missionaries in the foreign field when she heard steps on the broad stair that led down to the ample hall. A second later her husband appeared at the door with a young woman on his arm—a young woman who wore a hat with a red feather. This picture had hardly limned itself upon her acute intelligence before she saw, just behind her husband and the strange girl, a broad-shouldered young clergyman who bore himself quite as though accustomed to appearing unannounced in strange houses.

The banker stepped forward, shook hands with the bishop cordially, and carried off the introductions breezily.

"Sorry to be late, Gertie; but you know how it is!" Whereas, as a matter of fact, Mrs. Burgess did not know at all how it was. "Bishop, these young people wish to be married. Their time is short, as they have a train to make. Just how they came to be here is a long story, and it will have to wait. If you see anything familiar in Mr. Drake's clothes please don't be distressed, I've always intended doing something for your new cathedral, and you shall have a check and the price of a new suit early in the morning. And, Gertie"—he looked at his watch—"if you will find a prayerbook we can proceed to business."

Mrs. Burgess always marveled at her husband's plausibility, and now she had fresh proof of it. She blinked as he addressed the girl as Nellie; but this was just like Web Burgess!

The Bishop of Shoshone, having married cowboys and Indians in all manner of circumstances in his rough diocese, calmly began the service.

At the supper table they were all very merry except Nellie, whose face, carefully watched by Mrs. Burgess, grew grave at times—and once her eyes filled with tears; her young bridegroom spoke hardly at all. Burgess and the bishop, however, talked cheerfully of old times together, and they rose finally amid the laughter evoked by one of the bishop's stories. Burgess said he thought it would be nice if they all went to the station to give the young people a good sendoff for their long journey; and afterward they could look in at a concert, for which he had tickets, and hear Sembrich sing.

"After a busy day," he remarked, meeting Nellie's eyes at one of her tearful moments, "there's nothing like a little music to quiet the nerves—and this has been the greatest day of my life!"

VI

The president of the White River National Bank was late in reaching his desk the next morning. When he crossed the lobby he limped slightly; and his secretary, in placing the mail before him, noticed a strip

of plaster above his left ear. His "Good morning!"
was very cheery and he plunged into work with his
usual energy.

He had dictated a telegram confirming a bond deal
that would net him fifty thousand dollars, when his
name was spoken by a familiar voice. Swinging round
to the railing with calculated deliberation he addressed
his visitor in the casual tone established by their
intimacy:

"Hello, Hill—looking for me?"

"Nope; not yet!"

Both men grinned as their eyes met.

"Has the charming Miss Murdock been in this
morning?" asked the detective, glancing toward the
tellers' cages.

"Haven't seen her yet. Hope you're not infatuated
with the girl."

"Only in what you might call an artistic sense;
I think we agreed yesterday that she's rather pleasing
to the jaded eyesight. See the papers?"

"What's in the papers?" asked the banker, feeling
absently for a report a clerk had laid on his desk.

"Oh, a nice little muss out on Vevay Street last
night! The cops made a mess of it of course. Old
Murdock's son Bob shot a constable in Kentucky and
broke for the home plate to get some money, and I'd
had a wire to look out for him when I was in here
yesterday. He handled some very clever phony money
in this district a while back. I went out to Vevay
Street to take a look at him—and found the police
had beat me to it! The cash Nellie drew yesterday
was for him."

"Of course you got him!"

"No," said Hill; "he made a getaway, all right. It
was rather funny though——"

"How funny?"

"The chase he gave us. ·You don't mean you haven't heard about it!"

Burgess clasped his hands behind his head and yawned.

"I've told you repeatedly, Hill, that I don't read criminal news. It would spoil the fun of hearing you explain your own failures."

"Well, I won't bore you with this. I only want you to understand that it was the police who made a fluke of it. But I can't deny those Murdocks do interest me a good deal."

He bent his keen eyes upon the banker for a second and grinned. Burgess returned the grin.

"I've got to speak before the Civic League on our municipal government to-morrow night, and I'll throw something about the general incompetence of our police force—it's undoubtedly rotten!"

The detective lingered.

"By-the-way, I nearly overlooked this. Seems to be a silver card-case, with your name neatly engraved on the little tickets inside. I picked it up on the ice last night when I was skating on the canal. I'm going to keep one of the cards as a souvenir."

"Perfectly welcome, Tom. You'd better try one of these cigars."

Hill chose a cigar with care from the extended box and lighted it. Burgess swung round to his desk, turned over some letters, and then looked up as though surprised to find the detective still there.

"Looking for me, Tom?"

"No; not yet!"

THE CAMPBELLS ARE COMING

I

IT is not to be counted against Mrs. Robert Fleming Ward that at forty-five she had begun to look backward a little wistfully and forward a little disconsolately and apprehensively. She was a good woman, indeed one of the best of women, loyal, conscientious and self-sacrificing in the highest degree. But she was poignantly aware that certain ambitions dear to her heart had not been realized. Robert Fleming Ward had not attained that high place at the Sycamore County bar which had been his goal, and he seemed unable to pull himself to the level with Canby Taylor and Addison Swiggart who practiced in federal jurisdictions and were not unknown to the docket of the United States Supreme Court.

Even as Mrs. Ward was a good woman, so her husband Robert was a good man and a good lawyer. But just being good wasn't getting the Wards anywhere. At least it wasn't landing them within the golden portals of their early dreams. To find yourself marking time professionally and socially in a town of seventy-five thousand souls, that you've seen grow from twenty-five thousand, is a disagreeable experience if you are a sensitive person. And Mrs. Ward was sensitive. It grieved her to witness the prosperity flaunted by people like the Picketts, the Shepherds, the Kirbys and others comparatively new to the community, who

had impudently availed themselves of Sycamore
County's clay to make brick, and of its water power to
turn the wheels of industries for which the old time
Kernville pioneer stock had gloomily predicted failure.

The Picketts, the Shepherds, the Kirbys and the rest
of the new element had builded themselves houses
that were much more comfortable and pleasing to the
eye than the houses of the children and grandchildren
of the old families that had founded Kernville away
back when Madison was president.   The heads of the
respective brick, box, match, bottle, canning, and
strawboard industries might be deficient in culture but
they did employ good architects.   The Wards lived in
a house of the Queen Anne period, which it had been
necessary to mortgage to send John Marshall through
college and give Helen a year at a Connecticut finishing
school.   The Wards' home had deteriorated to the
point of dinginess, and the dinginess, and the inability
to keep a car, or to return social favors, or belong to
the new country club weighed heavily upon Mrs. Ward.

Her husband, with all his industry and the fine
talents she knew him to possess, was making no more
money at forty-seven than he had made at thirty-five.
She was a little bewildered to find that socially she
had gradually lost contact with the old aristocracy
without catching step with the flourishing makers of
brick and other articles of commerce that were carrying
the fame of Kernville into new territory.   And as
Mrs. Ward was possessed of a pardonable pride, this
situation troubled her greatly.   They had been unable
to send John to the Harvard Law School, but he had
made a fine record in the school of the state university,
and his name now appeared beneath his father's on
the door of the law office on the second floor of the old

Wheatley block, which had been pretty well deserted by tenants now that Kernville boasted a modern ten-story office building.

John Ward was a healthy, sanguine young fellow who had every intention of getting on. Some of the friends he had made in law school threw him some business, and it was remarked about the courthouse that John had more punch than his father, and was bound to succeed. Half way through the trial of a damage suit in which the firm of Ward & Ward represented a plaintiff who had been run down by an interurban car, the senior Ward was laid up with tonsilitis, and John carried the case through and won a verdict for twice what the plaintiff had been led to believe he could possibly get.

Helen Ward was quite as admirable and interesting as her brother. The finishing school had done her no harm and she returned to Kernville without airs, assumptions or affectations, understanding perfectly that her parents had done the best they could for her. She was nineteen, tall and straight, fair, with an abundance of brown hair and blue-gray mirthful eyes. The growing inability of her mother to maintain a maid-of-all work, now that Kernville's eligibles for domestic service preferred the eight-hour day of the factories to house work, did not trouble Helen particularly. She could cook, wash, iron, cut out a dress and sew it together and if the furniture was wobbly and the upholstery faded she was an artist with the glue-pot and her linen covers on the chairs gave the parlor a fresh smart look. The humor that was denied their parents was Helen's and John's portion in large measure. They were of the Twentieth Century, spoke its language and knew all its signs and symbols.

They were proud of each other, shared their pleasures and consoled each other in their disappointments, and resolutely determined to make the best of a world that wasn't such a bad place after all.

John reached home from the office on a day early in January and found Helen preparing supper.

"Great scott, sis; has that last girl faded already!"

"Skipped, vamoosed, vanished!" Helen answered, looking up from the gas range on which she was broiling a steak. "The offer of a dollar more a week transferred her to the Kirby's, where she'll have nothing to do but cook. The joke's on them. She's the worst living cook, and not even a success in hiding her failures."

"I hope," said John, helping himself to a stalk of celery and biting it meditatively, "I hope the Kirbys suffer the most frightful tortures before they die of indigestion. Haven't invited us to the party they're giving, have they?"

"Not unless our invitations got lost in the mails. And I hear it's going to be a snappy function with the refreshments and a jazz band imported from Chicago."

"Look here, sis, that's rubbing it in pretty hard! I don't care for myself, but it's nasty of 'em to cut you. But in a way it's an act of reprisal. Mother didn't ask Mrs. Kirby and Jeannette to the tea she threw for that national federation swell just before Christmas. But even at that——"

"Oh, don't be so analytical! We're an old family and mama refuses to see any merit in people whose grandparents didn't settle here before the Indians left. And as we haven't the money to train with the ancient aristocracy, we've got to huddle on the side lines. Pardon me, dear, but that's a pound of butter you're about to sit on! You might cut a slice and place it neatly on yonder plate."

"Snobbery!" said John, as he cut the butter with exaggerated deliberation;—"snobbery is a malady, a disease. You can't kill it; you've got to feed it its own kind of pabulum. It's as plain as daylight that we've got to do something to get out of the hole or we're stuck for good."

"We might bore for oil in the back yard," said Helen, scrutinizing the steak. "If we struck a gusher we could break into the country club and buy a large purple limousine like the Kirbys."

"My professional engagements don't exhaust my brain power at present, and I'm giving considerable thought to ways and means of improving our state, condition or status as a family of exalted but unrecognized merit."

"You're doing nobly, John! Tom Reynolds told me they were talking of running you for prosecuting attorney. That would give you a grand boost. And there's Alice Hovey,—I understand all about that, John. I think you're mistaken about the Hoveys not liking you."

"Ah, Alice!" he exclaimed mockingly. "Papa and mama Hovey have quite other ideas for Alice; no penniless barrister need apply! But I won't deny to you that I'm pretty keen about Alice, only when I go to the house the fond parents create a low temperature that is distinctly chilly. Listen to me, Helen," he went on with an abrupt change of tone. "You and Ned Shepherd were hitting it off grandly when something happened. He's a fine chap and I rather got the idea that you two would make a match of it."

"Oh no!" she protested, quickly but unconvincingly as she transferred the steak to the platter.

"His family's trying to switch him to Sally Pickett. He hasn't been here lately, but you do see him occasionally?"

There were tears in her eyes as she swung round from the range.

"I've got to stop that, John! I'm ashamed of myself for meeting him as I've been doing—walking with him in the back streets and letting him talk to me over the telephone when mama isn't round. I didn't know——"

"Well, I just happened to spot you Monday evening, and I meant to speak to you about it. Not exactly nice, sis. I'm sorry about the whole business. Ned's really a manly chap, and I don't believe he'll be bullied into giving you up."

"All over now, John," she answered with badly-feigned indifference.

"Well, the course of true love never did run smooth. Father and mother have done their almighty best for us, but changes have come so fast in this burg they haven't been able to keep up with the procession. Father misses chances now and then, as in refusing the Pickett case when the State went after him for polluting the river with refuse from his strawboard mill. Dad thought the prosecution was justified and foolishly volunteered to assist the State as a public duty. Pickett lost and had to spend a lot of money changing his plant; so he's knocked us whenever he got a chance."

"That's just like papa. I only wish we could do something really splendid for him and mama."

"We're going to, sis," said John confidently. "Take it from me we're going to do that identical thing.

Now give me the potatoes and the coffee-pot. Precede me with the bread and butter. There's mother at the front door now. Step high as to the strains of a march of triumph. We'll give a fine exhibition of a happy family, one for all and all for one!"

II

Mrs. Ward, detained by a club committee meeting, began to apologize for not getting home in time to assist with the supper.

"Oh, John did all the heavy work! And we had a fine talk into the bargain," Helen replied cheerfully.

As her father was tired and didn't know the latest domestic had departed hence, she went on with an ironic description of the frailties and incapacity of that person and pictured the gloom of the Kirbys as they ate her initial meal. Mrs. Ward had brought the afternoon mail to the table. She was the corresponding secretary of a state federation which used the mails freely. She ate in silence, absorbed in her letters, while her husband praised Helen's cooking.

Ward found a real joy in his children. It was not lost upon him that they were making the best of circumstances for which in a somewhat bewildered fashion he felt himself responsible. Their very kindness, their disposition to make the best of things, hurt him and deepened his growing sense of defeat. John began talking of a case they were to try shortly. He had found some decisions that supported the contention of their client. They were explaining it to Helen, who teased them by perversely taking the opposite view, when they were silenced by an exclamation from Mrs. Ward.

"Here's news indeed! This is a note from Mrs. Campbell, the Ruth Sanders who was my best friend at school,—Mrs. Walter Scott Campbell," she added impressively, looking round at them over her glasses. "It's short; I'll just read it:

"DEAREST IPHIGENIA:—

("You know the girls at Miss Woodburn's school always called me Iphigenia—due to a stupid answer I once gave in the literature class.)

> "It's so sweet of you to remember me year after year with a Christmas card. The very thought of you always brings up all the jolly times we had at Miss Woodburn's. We parted with a promise to meet every year; and I have never set eyes on you since we sat side by side at the closing exercises! The class letter doesn't come around any more, but your children must be grown up. Mine are very much so and getting married and leaving Walter and me quite forlorn.

("Her daughter Angela married into that Thornton family of Rhode Island—or maybe it was the Connecticut branch—who are so terribly rich; made it in copper; no, I believe it was rubber.)

> "Don't be startled, but Mr. Campbell and I are planning to go to California next month, and as we have to pass right across your state, it seems absurd not to stop and see you. I've looked up the time tables and we can easily leave the Limited at Cleveland and run down to Kernville. Now don't go to any trouble for us, but treat us just as old friends and if it isn't convenient to stay with you for a night—we just must have a night to gossip about the old days—we can put up at the

hotel. We shan't leave here until February 17, but wishing to acknowledge your card— I never can remember to send Christmas cards —I thought I'd give you fair warning of our approach. Always, dear Iphigenia, your affectionate,   RUTH."

"That's a charming letter!" Helen volunteered, as her mother's gaze invited approval of Mrs. Campbell's graciousness in promising a visit. "She must be lovely!"

"Ruth was the dearest of all my girlhood friends! When she had typhoid and her family were in Europe I was able to do little things for her;—nothing really of importance—but she has never forgotten. She was so appreciative and generous and always wanted her friends to share her good times!"

All their lives John and Helen had heard their mother sing the praises of Mrs. Walter Scott Campbell, née Sanders, until that lady had assumed something of the splendor of a mythical figure in their imaginations. She had been the richest girl in the Hudson River school Mrs. Ward had attended, and she had married wealth. The particular Campbell of her choice had inherited a fortune which he had vastly augmented. When occasionally a New York newspaper drifted into the house Mrs. Ward scanned the financial advertisements for the name of Walter Scott Campbell set out in bold type as the director of the most august institutions.

"I suppose——" Mrs. Ward's tone expressed awe in all its connotations;—"I suppose Mr. Campbell is worth fifty million at the lowest calculation. I met him years ago at one of the school dances. He was quite wild about Ruth then, and they were married, John, just a year before we were. I still have the invitation, and Ruth sent me a piece of the wedding cake. And from the photograph she sent me at Christmas two years ago, I judge that time has dealt lightly with her."

"Campbell's one of the most important men in Wall Street," Ward assented. "One of his institutions, The Sutphen Loan & Trust, financed the Kernville Water Power Company, a small item of course for so big a concern. Campbell probably never heard of it."

"Well, men of his calibre usually know where the dollars go," said John, whose wits were functioning rapidly.

"Of course we simply can't let them go to the hotel," continued Mrs. Ward; "the Kipperly House is a disgrace. And if Ruth hasn't changed a lot in twenty-six years she'll accept us as she finds us. Our guest room needs redecorating, and we can hardly keep the jackets on the parlor furniture right in the middle of winter; and the bath-room fixtures ought to be replaced——"

She paused, seeing the look of dejection on her husband's face. He was well aware that all these things were old needs which the coming of important guests now made imperative. Mrs. Ward carefully thrust the note back into its envelope. John exchanged telegraphic glances with Helen. His eyes brightened with the stress of his thoughts but he buttered a bit of bread before he spoke.

"Well, mother," he began briskly, "I'm sure we're all tickled that your old friend's coming. I can just see you sitting up all night talking of the midnight spreads you had, and how you fooled the teachers. Now don't worry about the house—you or father, either; I'm going to manage that."

"But, John, we mustn't add to your father's worries. I realize perfectly that we're in debt and can't spend money we haven't got. Ruth was always a dear—so considerate of everyone—and we'll hope it's me and my family and not the house she's coming to see."

"That's all right, mother, but this strikes me as something more than a casual visit. I see in it the hand of Providence!" he cried eagerly.

"If they carry a maid and valet as part of their scenery we're lost—hopelessly lost!" Helen suggested.

"Oh, not necessarily!" John replied. "We'll stow 'em away somewhere. In a pinch, you and I can move to the attic. Anyhow, we've got a month to work in. When we begin to get publicity for the coming of the rich and distinguished Campbells, I miss my guess if things don't begin to look a lot easier."

"But, John," his mother began, shaking her head with disapproval, "you wouldn't do anything that would look—vulgar?"

"Certainly not, but the Sunday *Journal's* always keen for news of impending visitors in our midst, and no people of the Campbells' social and financial standing have ever honored our city with their presence. The president of the Transcontinental did park his private car in the yards last summer, but before the Chamber of Commerce could tackle him about building a new freight house he faded away."

"Walter Scott Campbell is a director in the Transcontinental," remarked Mrs. Ward. "I happened to see his name in the list when I looked up the name of the company's secretary to send on the resolutions of the Women's Municipal Union complaining of the vile condition of the depot."

"Such matters are never passed on in the New York

offices," Ward suggested mildly. "Our business organizations have worked on the General Manager for years without getting anywhere."

"Just a word from a man of Mr. Campbell's power will be enough," replied John spaciously. "For another thing the train schedule ought to be changed to give us a local sleeper to Chicago. We'll stir up the whole service of the Transcontinental when we get Walter here!"

"Walter!" exclaimed Mrs. Ward, aghast at this familiarity.

"Better call him Walt, John, to make him feel at home," suggested Helen.

"The directors of the Water Power Company want to refund their bonds. I suppose Mr. Campbell could help about that," Ward remarked, interested in spite of himself in the potentialities of the impending visit.

"But it would be a betrayal of hospitality," Mrs. Ward protested, "and we mustn't do anything to spoil their visit."

"Oh, that visit's going to be a great thing for Kernville! It grows on me the more I think of it," said John loftily. "It's our big chance to do something for the town. And the Campbells can't object. They will pass on, never knowing the vast benefits they have conferred upon mankind."

"Your imagination's running away with you, John," said his father. "With only one day here to renew their acquaintance with your mother they'll hardly care to be dragged through the factories and over the railway yards."

"While mother and Helen are entertaining Mrs. Campbell, we'll borrow the largest car in town and show Walter the sights. And it will be up to us to

prove to him that Kernville's the best little town of
the seventy-five thousand class in the whole rich valley
of the Mississippi. All Walter will have to do will be
to send a few wires in a casual manner to the right
parties and everything the town needs will be forth-
coming."

"But why should we worry about the town when it
isn't worrying particularly about us?" asked Helen as
she began to clear the table.

"I don't quite follow you either," said his mother.
"You can't, you really mustn't——"

"Such matters are for the male of the species to
grapple with. You and Helen arrange a tea or dinner
or whatever you please, making something small and
select of the function, and I'll do all the rest."

"In some way John and I will manage the money,"
said Mr. Ward, slowly, and then catching a meaning-
ful look in John's eyes, he added with unwonted confidence: "Where there's a will there's a way. I want
the Campbells' visit to be a happy occasion. You are
entitled to it, Margaret—you and Helen must get all
the pleasure possible from meeting a woman of Mrs.
Campbell's large experience of life."

"Mama will need a new frock," said Helen, a remark
which precipitated at once a lively debate with her
mother as to which if any item of her existing wardrobe would lend itself to the process of reconstruction.
This question seemed susceptible of endless discussion,
and was only ended by John's firm declaration that
there should be new raiment for both his mother and
Helen.

"Father, we'll show these upstarts from New York
what real American women are like!"

"We shall be ruined!" cried Helen tragically, as she

disappeared through the swing door with a pile of plates.

"Please, John, don't do anything foolish," his mother pleaded, but she smiled happily under the compulsion of his enthusiasm.

"Trust me for that!" he replied, laying his hands on her shoulders. "We're all too humble; that's what's the matter with the Ward family. And for once I want you to step right out!"

He waved her into the sitting room and darted into the kitchen, where he threw off his coat and donned an apron.

III

"Crazy! You've gone plumb stark crazy!" said Helen, as she thrust her arms into the dishwater. "It's cruel to raise mother's hopes that way. You know well enough that as things are going we're just about getting by, with the grocery bill two months behind and that eternal interest on the mortgage hanging over us like the well-known sword of Damocles."

"The sword is in my hands!" declared John, balancing a plate on the tip of his finger. "How does that old tune go?

> The Campbells are coming, tra la, tra la,
> The Campbells are coming, tra la!

There's a bit of Scotch in us, and I feel my blood tingle to those blithe martial strains! What's the rule for drying dishes, sis? Do you make 'em shine like a collar from a Chinese laundry, or is the dull domestic finish in better form?"

"If you break that plate I'll poison your breakfast coffee! If I didn't know you for a sober boy I'd think you'd been keeping tryst with a bootlegger! You don't seem to understand that you sat there at the table spending money like Midas on a spree. You couldn't borrow a cent if you tried!"

"Borrow!" he mocked. "I'm going to pull this thing off according to specifications, and I'm not going to borrow a cent. I expect to be refusing offers of money gently but firmly within a week. Observe my smoke, dearest one! Watch my fleet sail right up to the big dam in Sycamore River laden like the ships of Tarshish that brought gifts of silver and gold and ivory, apes and peacocks for Solomon's delight!"

"You're not calling the Campbells apes and peacocks!"

"Not on your life! All those rich treasures will be yours and mine, O Helen of Kernville! The Campbells are rich enough. We're not going to embarrass them by piling any more wealth on 'em. But the magic of the name of Walter Scott Campbell, if properly invoked, manipulated and flaunted will put us all on the high road to fame and fortune."

"You'll break mama's heart if you begin bragging about her acquaintance with this woman she hasn't seen for a quarter of a century! She's already warned you against vulgar boasting."

"Keep mother busy planning for the care and entertainment of our guests! I'll hold father steady. This being Thursday I've got time enough to plan the campaign before Sunday. I'll lay down a barrage and throw myself upon the enemy. To the cheering strains of 'The Campbells are Coming!' we'll cross the valley of death and plant our flag on the battlements without a scratch or the loss of a man."

By the time the kitchen was in order he had her

laughing and quite won to his idea that it was perfectly legitimate to avail themselves fully of the great opportunity offered by the Campbells' visit.

"Nothing undignified at all! The Campbells will never be conscious of my proceedings as they don't read the Kernville papers and will linger only a day. By the way, it happens that Billy Townley, a fraternity brother of mine, has just been made city editor of the *Journal* and Billy and I used to pull some good stunts when we were together at the 'varsity. When I hiss the password in his ear and tell him I'll need a little space daily for a few weeks he'll go right down the line for me. And the boys on the *Evening Sun* are friends of mine, too. They have less space but they make up for it with bigger headlines."

"You're a dear boy, John, if you are crazy! I believe you can do most anything you tackle, and I'll stand by you whether you land us in jail or in the poorhouse."

"Bully for you, sis!" And then lowering his voice, "This chance may never come again! I'm going to wring every possible drop out of it even as you wring out that dish rag. By the way, if it isn't impertinent, when did you see Ned last?"

"Not since the day you saw me walking with him— for the last time. But he telephoned this afternoon. He wanted to come up this evening."

"Well, he's of age and the curfew law can't touch him. What was the answer?"

"I told him I wouldn't be at home. I'm not going to have him calling here when his mother barely speaks to me! Ned didn't say so, but I suspect she gave him a good scolding for taking me instead of Sally to the Seebrings' dance."

"How do you get that? If he didn't tell you——!"

"Of course not! But Sally had to go with her mother and there were more girls than men; so Sally only had about half the dances and the rest of the time sat on the sidelines with her mother and Mrs. Kirby. I caught a look now and then that was quite suggestive of murder in the first degree."

"Helen," said John, lifting his eyes dreamily to the ceiling, "I'll wager a diamond tiara against one of your delicious buckwheat cakes that you and I will get an invitation to the Kirby party."

"Taken! The cards went out yesterday. I met some of the girls down town this morning, and they were buzzing about it."

"Let 'em buzz! Ours will probably come special delivery with a note of explanation that in copying the list or something of the kind we were regrettably omitted. And let me see," he went on, rubbing his chin reflectively, "I rather think Ned will ask you to go to the party with him. It occurs to me that old man Shepherd owns some land he's trying to sell to the Transcontinental, and the railway people are shy of it because it's below the flood line on our perverse river. Yes; I think we may jar the Shepherds a little too."

"Why, John!" she laughed as she hung up her apron, "you almost persuade me that you've already got free swing at the Campbell boodle!"

"I look at it this way, Helen. We can all spend our own money; it's getting the benefit of other people's money that requires genius. I must now step down to the public library and to the *Journal* office to get some dope on the Campbells. Also I'll have to sneak mother's photograph of Mrs. Campbell out of the house. A few illustrations will give tone to our publicity stuff."

"Be bold, John, but not too bold!"

"'The Campbells are coming, tra la!'" he sang mockingly, and seizing her hands, hummed the air and danced back and forth across the kitchen. "By jing, that tune's wonderful for the toddle!" he cried exultantly. "We'll make all Kernville step to it."

IV

"The point we want to hammer in is that we— the Ward family—are the only people in Sycamore county who are in touch with the Campbell power, social and financial," John elucidated to his friend Townley. "Modest, retiring to the point of utter self-effacement as we, the Wards, are, no other family in the community has ever been honored by a visit from so big a bunch of assets. And when it comes to social prominence their coming will link Kernville right on to Newport where old Walter Scott Campbell owns one of the lordliest villas. Here's a picture of it I found in 'Summer Homes of Great Americans.' We'll feed in the pictorial stuff from time to time, using this photograph of Mrs. Campbell mother keeps on the upright at home, and that cut of Walter Scott I dug out of your office graveyard. Your record shows you ran it the time the old money-devil was indicted under the Sherman law for conspiracy against the peace and dignity of the United States in a fiendish attempt to boost the price of bathtubs. The indictment was quashed as to the said Walter because he was laid up with whooping cough when the wicked attack on the free ablutions of the American people was planned or concocted, and he denied all responsibility for the acts of his proxy."

"You've got to hand it to that lad," said Townley

ruminatively. "Anything you can do to put me in the way of a soft snap as private secretary for his majesty would be appreciated. I've had considerable experience in keeping my friends out of jail and I might be of use to him."

John rose early on Sunday morning to inspect his handiwork in the section of the *Journal* devoted to the goings and comings, the entertainments past and prospective and the club activities of Kernville. Townley had eliminated the usual group of portraits of the brides of the week that Mrs. Walter Scott Campbell's handsome countenance might be spread across three columns in the center of the page. The photograph of Mrs. Campbell had been admirably reproduced, and any one informed in such matters would know instantly that she was the sort of woman who looks well in evening gowns and that her pearl necklace was of unquestionable authenticity.

The usual double column "lead" was devoted wholly to the announcement of the visit of the Walter Scott Campbells of New York and Newport to the Robert Fleming Wards of Kernville, with all biographical data necessary to establish the Campbells in the minds of intelligent readers as persons of indubitable eminence entitled to the most distinguished consideration in every part of the world. Mrs. Campbell, John had learned from "Distinguished American Women," was a Mayflower descendant, a Colonial Dame and a Daughter of the Revolution, besides being a trustee of eighteen separate and distinct philanthropies, and all these matters were impressively set forth. Mr. Campbell's clubs in town and country required ten lines for their recital. Any jubilation over the coming of so much magnificence was neatly concealed under the generalization that the horizon of Kernville was rapidly widening and that there was bound to be more and more communication between New York and Kernville. Mrs. Ward, the article concluded, had not yet decided in just what manner she would entertain for the Campbells, but the representative people of the city would undoubtedly have an opportunity to meet her guests.

"The first gun is fired!" John whispered, thrusting the paper through Helen's bed-room door. "Read and ponder well!"

Mrs. Ward read the announcement aloud at the breakfast table as soberly as though it were a new constitution for her favorite club.

"That Miss Givens who does the society news for the *Journal* has more sense than I gave her credit for," she said. "There isn't a word in that piece that isn't true. But that portrait of Ruth is a trifle too large; you ought to have warned them about that! When Tetrazzini sang here they didn't print her picture half as big as that."

"Well, mother, the *Journal* simply begged for a photograph. People of note don't mind publicity. They simply eat it up!"

"Well, the article is really very nice," said Mrs. Ward, "but I hope they won't say anything more until the Campbells arrive."

John, aware that several columns more bearing upon the Campbell visit were already in type in the *Journal* office, was grateful to Helen for changing the subject to a pertinent discussion of the proper shade of wall paper for the guest room.

On Tuesday the *Journal's* first page contained a news-article on the crying need of enlarged railway facilities, adroitly written to embody the hope of the transportation committee of the Chamber of Commerce, that when Mr. Walter Scott Campbell of the board of directors of the Transcontinental paid his expected visit to the city he would take steps to change the reactionary policy of the road's operating department. The same article stated with apparent authority that Robert Fleming Ward, the well-known attorney, whose guest Mr. Campbell would be, had pledged himself to assist the mayor and the Chamber of Commerce to the utmost in urging Kernville's needs upon the great capitalist.

"See here, John, you've got to be careful about this Campbell business!" Mr. Ward's tone was severe. "I know without your telling me you inspired that piece in this morning's paper. Campbell never saw me in his life and that article gives the impression that he and I are old cronies. It's going to cause us all a lot of embarrassment. It won't do!"

"Sorry if it bothers you, father; but there's nothing untrue in that article. You'll be the only man in town who can get Campbell's ear. If he refuses to interest himself in a new freight house and that sort of thing, that's his affair."

The stenographer knocked to announce Mr. Pickett.

"Say to him," replied John, indifferently, "that we are in conference but he can see us in just a moment."

"Pickett!" exclaimed Ward, senior, as the door closed. "What on earth brings him here!"

"The Campbells are coming," replied John with a grin. "Pickett's president of the Water Power Company, and he wants to line us up to get Campbell interested in making a new bond deal."

"Humph! If that's what he wants I like his nerve. We don't even speak when we meet."

"You'll be speaking now! Let's go out and give him the glad hand of brotherly greeting."

A little diffident at first, Wesley T. Pickett warmed under the spell of the Wards' magnanimity.

"I've regretted very much our little differences——" he began.

"There's no feeling on our side at all, Mr. Pickett," John declared and his father, a little dazed, murmured his acquiescence in this view of the matter, and eyed with interest a formidable bundle of documents in Pickett's hands.

"Fact is," remarked Pickett, with a sheepish grin as he re-crossed his legs, "you were dead right on that matter of the pollution of the river. Swiggert probably did the best he could with our defense but you were right when you told me I'd save money and avoid arousing hostile feeling in the community by pleading guilty."

"It's always disagreeable to be obliged to tell a man he hasn't a good case," Ward announced.

"Well, I want you to know I respect you for your honesty. Swiggert encouraged me to think he might get us off on some technical defect in the statute, and it cost me a two thousand dollar fee to find he was wrong."

"The point he raised was an interesting one," Ward remarked mildly, "and he might have made it stick."

"But he didn't!" Pickett retorted a little savagely. "Now I got a matter I want the God's truth about, absolutely. It's a row I've got into with a few of my stockholders in the glass company. The fools got the idea of freezing me out! It's all in these papers, and I want you to give it all the time it needs, but I want an opinion,—no more than you can get on a letter sheet. Swiggert uses too many words and I've got to have a yes or no."

The thought of being frozen out caused Mr. Pickett to swell with indignation. He turned from father to son in an unvoiced but eloquent appeal to be saved from so monstrous and impious an assault upon his dignity.

"Certainly, Mr. Pickett," said the senior Ward, accepting the papers. "We'll be glad to take up the matter. It's possible I may have to ask some questions——"

"That will be all right, Ward! I don't mind telling you I'm a good deal worried about this thing. I'm at the Elks Club most every noon, and if you'll just 'phone when you're ready to see me we can have lunch together. Now, I guess a retainer's the usual thing. What do you say to a thousand or two?"

John with difficulty refrained from screaming that two would be much more to the taste of the firm, but his father's gentle and slightly tremulous murmur that one thousand would be satisfactory stilled him. The check written with a flourish, lay on the edge of Ward senior's desk while Pickett abused the enemies who were trying to wrest from him the control of the glass company.

"I'm familiar with the general question you indicate," said Ward, senior; "I went into it a while back in a similar case for a client in Newton county; we shall give it our best attention."

"I got confidence in you!" blurted Pickett. "That's why I brought the job here." He thrust a big cigar into his mouth and began feeling in his pocket for a match which John instantly supplied.

"Notice by the paper," remarked Pickett, "that Campbell of the Transcontinental's comin' out. If you could arrange it, I'd like a chance to talk to him about the Water Power bonds the Sutphen Trust's handled for us. I went to New York a couple of weeks ago to see about refunding and I couldn't get near anybody but the fourth vice president. Wouldn't want to bother you, but if I could just get a chance at Campbell and show him the plant——"

"I'm sure that can be arranged very easily," John answered quickly, noting a look of apprehension on his father's face. "It will be a pleasure to arrange a meeting for you."

"I'd particularly appreciate it," said Pickett, shaking hands with both of them; and John accompanied him to the head of the stairway, where they shook hands again.

"You don't think," asked Ward, senior, looking up from Pickett's papers, which he had already spread out on his desk,—"you don't really think the Campbells had anything to do with this——"

"Not a thing, dad!" John replied gaily. "I'll just call up Helen and tell her to go ahead with the redecorating and other things necessary to put our house in order for royalty!"

John had deposited Pickett's check and was crossing the lobby of the Kernville National when he met Jason V. Kirby leaving the officers' corner.

"Hello, John!" exclaimed the brick manufacturer affably. "Haven't seen you round much of late. Funny I ran into you; just going up to see you. You know Taylor's my lawyer, but he's in Chicago trying

a long case, and I got an abstract of title I'm in a
hurry to have examined.   Glad if you or your father
would pass on it.   Farm I'm buying out in Decatur
township."

"Certainly, Mr. Kirby; we can give it immediate
attention," John replied as though it were a common
occurrence for him to pick up business in this fashion.

To Kirby's suggestion that if he didn't mind he
might walk over to the brick company's office and get
the abstract, John answered that he didn't mind in
the least.   The abstract was bulky, and John roughly
estimated that a report on it would be worth at least
a hundred dollars.   Kirby explained that the land was
needed for the extension of the brick business and that
he had taken a ten-day option to keep a rival company
from picking it up.

"Look here, John," remarked Kirby carelessly, as
John started off with the abstract in his pocket, "I see
that the Campbells are coming out to visit your folks.
Don't let 'em overlook Kirby brick.   We're reachin'
right out for New York business."

"Certainly, Mr. Kirby.   Father has it in mind to
take Mr. Campbell for an inspection of all our industries, and I'll give you the tip so you can be all set to
show off your plant."

"Occurs to me Campbell might make a short speech
to our workmen; just a nice friendly jolly, you understand."

"That will be perfectly simple, Mr. Kirby.   Trust
me to arrange it."

V

When John and his father reached home, Helen fell
upon her brother's neck.

"I've lost that wager! We're invited!"

"Ah! The poison is at work, is it? Did it come special post, or did their dusky Senegambian bear the cards hither upon a golden plate?"

"Neither! Mrs. Kirby and Jeannette called and left them personally. I was making bread when they arrived but I had the presence of mind to shed my apron on my way to the door to let them in. Mother was darning socks but she came down and they stayed so long the bread burned to a cinder."

"A few loaves of bread are nothing—nothing!"

"But, John, dear, I think maybe——" began Mrs. Ward, uncertainly and paused, noting that her husband was emptying a satchel of important looking papers as though he expected to spend the evening at work. He appeared more cheerful than she had seen him in years.

"Better let John have his way," said Ward, senior. "The Campbells are driving business into the office and we're not going to turn it away."

"It's your ability that's bringing the business; you've always been a bigger man than Taylor or Swiggert!" declared Mrs. Ward, when the day's events had been explained to her.

"We'll pretend that's it anyhow," Ward assented. "There's a mighty interesting question in that case of Pickett's. You may be sure I'm going to give it my best care."

"I'm so proud of you, Robert!"

"Be proud of John," he laughed; "the boy's bound to make or ruin us in these next few weeks."

It was astonishing the number of ways in which the prospective visit of the Campbells became a matter of deep concern to Kernville. Billy Townley had entered with zest into John's campaign, and Martin Cowdery, the owner of the *Journal* and the congressman from the district, wired instructions from Washington to cut things loose on the Campbell visit. Under the same potent inspiration the *Journal's* venerable editorial writer took a vacation from his regular business of explaining and defending the proprietor's failure to land a fish hatchery for the old Sycamore district and celebrated the approach of the Campbells under such captions as "The Dawn of a New Era," and "Stand up, Kernville." He called loudly upon the mayor, who was not of the *Journal's* politics, to clean the streets that their shameful condition might not offend the eyes and the nostrils of the man of millions who was soon to honor the city with his presence.

The *Sun*, not to be outdone, boldly declared that Campbell was coming to Kernville as the representative of interests that were seeking an eligible site for a monster steel casting plant, an imaginative flight that precipitated a sudden call for a meeting of the Bigger Kernville Committee of the Chamber of Commerce, and the expenditure of fifteen dollars with war tax to wire a set of resolutions to Walter Scott Campbell. A five-line dispatch in the press report announcing that Walter Scott Campbell had given half a million toward the endowment of a hospital in Honolulu was handled as a local item, quite as though Kernville alone vibrated to Campbell's generous philanthropies.

"Helen, we've got 'em going!" John chortled at the beginning of the second week. "Three automobile agents have offered me the biggest cars in their show rooms to carry the Campbells hither and yon. I'm encouraging competition for the honor. The Chamber

of Commerce wants to give a banquet with speeches
and everything for our old friend Walter. Old man
Shepherd climbed our stairs today, risking apoplexy at
every step, to ask as a special favor that the Chamber
be granted this high privilege."

"Ned's asked me to go to the Kirby party with
him," confessed Helen. "The embargo seems to be
off."

"Ha!" cried John dramatically. "Mrs. Hovey called
me up to request my presence at dinner Wednesday
night. Alice has a friend visiting her. Alice with the
hair so soft and so brown, as stated in the ballad, is
the dearest girl in the world next to you, sis; no snobbery about her; but her mama! Ah, mama has seen a
great light in the heavens!"

The population of Kernville was now divided into
two classes, those who would in all likelihood be per-
mitted to meet the Campbells, and those who could
hardly hope for this coveted privilege. The *Journal*
followed a picture of the Campbells' Newport villa,
fortified with a glowing description of its magnificence,
with a counterfeit presentment of the *White Gull*,
which had almost the effect of anchoring the Campbells' seagoing yacht in the muddy Sycamore at the
foot of Harrison street.

"The yacht's the biggest thing we've pulled yet,"
John announced to Helen, a few days after the craft's
outlines had been made familiar to the *Journal's* con-
stituency. "Since we sprung it our office has drawn
four good cases, not including the collection business
of the Tilford Casket Company, which ought to be
good for a thousand bucks a year if the death rate in
the rich valley of the Sycamore doesn't go down on us."

"It's wonderful, John!" said Helen, in an awed tone.

"Mrs. Montgomery spent an hour with mother this afternoon talking of the good old times, and how all us old families must stand together, and she insisted on throwing a tea for Mrs. Campbell—just for our old friends—you know how she talks! She'd no sooner rolled away than Mrs. Everett Crawford invaded our home and interfered terribly with the paper hangers while she begged to be allowed to give a dinner for the Campbells in the new home they've built with boodle they've made canning our native fruits."

"Splendid! There may be some business there before we get through with it! Young Freddie Crawford is the gayest of our joy riders, and it would be worth a big retainer to keep him out of the penal farm."

A second stenographer had been established in the office of Ward & Ward to care for the increased business when Cowdery left the halls of Congress for a look at his fences, held conferences with John in an upper room of the Kipperly House, sacred to political conspiracy, and caused the *Journal* forthwith to launch a boom for John Ward for prosecuting attorney subject to the decision of the April primaries.

"Look here, little brother," said Helen, coming in from a dance to which Ned Shepherd had taken her, and finding John in the sitting room at work on one of the new cases that had been bestowed upon Ward & Ward, "we've got to put on brakes."

"What's troubling you, sis? Isn't everybody treating you all right?"

"A queen couldn't receive more consideration! But what's worrying me is how we're ever going to satisfy these silly people. If all the plutocrats in New York should come to visit us we couldn't spread them around in a way to please all our fellow townsmen. We're certainly in the lime light! People were buzzing me tonight about the prosecutorship—say you'll win in a walk. But tell me what you think Cowdery's going to expect from you in return. Does he want to shake the Campbell cherry tree?"

John eyed her with philosophical resignation.

"Now that you've been enfranchised by the Nineteenth Amendment to the Constitution of this more or less free republic, you must learn to view matters with a mind of understanding. Cowdery hankers for a promotion to the senate. If the accursed money interests of the nation are persuaded that he is not a menace to the angels of Wall street they can sow some seed over the rich soil of this noble commonwealth that will be sure to bear fruit. There's a lot of Eastern capital invested in the state and a word carelessly spoken by the right persons, parties or groups in tall buildings in New York and a substantial corruption fund sent out from the same quarter will do much to help Cowdery through the primary. In me, sweet child, Cowdery sees a young man of great promise, who can hitch the powerful Campbell to his wagon."

"And if you can't do the hitching——?"

"Been giving thought to that, sis. Those resolutions the enterprising Bigger Kernville Committee sent Campbell annoy me a great deal. We can only hope that Walter has a sense of humor. The *Journal's* got a new untouched photograph of him from somewhere and the boy looks cheerful. He has a triple chin and there are lines around his eyes and mouth that argue for a mirthful nature. The rest, dearest, is on the knees of the gods!"

VI

It was in the third week of Mr. John Marshall Ward's vigorous campaign of education that Walter Scott Campbell, in his office in New York, tossed the last of the letters he had been answering to his stenographer and rang for his secretary.

A pale young man entered and waited respectfully for the magnate to look up from the newspaper clippings he was scanning.

"Parker, where the deuce did you get this stuff?" Campbell asked.

"They came in our usual press clipping service. Your order covers the better papers in the larger towns where you have interests. It's not often I find anything worth showing you."

"Well, don't let me miss anything like this!" replied Campbell with a chuckle.

He unfolded a page that had been sent complete, being indeed the society page of the Kernville *Morning Journal* of the previous Sunday. Campbell chuckled again, much to the relief of the pale secretary, who feared he might have brought to his employer's attention some news of evil omen. Campbell continued to read, chuckling as he rapidly turned over the cuttings.

"You look a little run down, Parker," he remarked affably. "A change of air would do you good. Give Miss Calderwood my calendar of appointments and any data I may need in the next few days, and take the first train for Kernville. Study this stuff carefully and find out what it's all about. There are some resolutions from the Kernville Chamber of Commerce about a site for a steel casting plant. Curious about that! Must have been a leak somewhere. We discussed possible locations in that secret conference at Pittsburgh last week, but Kernville wasn't mentioned. But that town, with its water power, might possibly be just right. Give it a looking over, but be very guarded in all your inquiries. And learn all you can about these Wards, father and son."

"Yes, Mr. Campbell," and Parker glanced at his watch.

"Mrs. Ward is an old friend of Mrs. Campbell—you understand. There's an old attachment and an obligation, as I remember. Mrs. Ward was exceedingly kind to Mrs. Campbell back in their school days when my wife was ill. She has never forgotten it."

"My inquiries as to the Wards are to be made in a sympathetic spirit? I understand, sir!"

"We are scheduled to stop at Kernville for a day on our way to California—is that right?"

"Yes, Mr. Campbell. Your car is ordered attached to the Transcontinental Limited leaving at five twenty-one on Tuesday, February seventeen."

"Take several days to this investigation. Learn what you can of these people, the town itself and so on. All this whoop and hurrah out there is unusual. Most amusing thing that's turned up since they wanted me to go out to some town in that neighborhood and preside at a barbecue. What place was that?"

"Scottsburg, Indiana, during the campaign of 1916," replied the invaluable Parker.

"A great people, those of the Middle West," remarked Mr. Campbell reflectively. "As the phrase goes, you've got to hand it to them. That's all, Parker."

Mr. Elwell Parker had frequently played the role of confidential investigator for Walter Scott Campbell,

and established the following evening at the Kipperly
House he began his labors with his usual intelligence,
thoroughness and discretion. Within twenty-four hours
there was little pertaining to the Wards, the social or
business conditions of Kernville that he did not know.
Twenty-four hours more sufficed for his complete en-
lightenment as to the thriving city's advantages as a
manufacturing point, the value and possibilities of its
water power, and the financial and moral status of its
leading citizens. He thereupon wrote a report, con-
densed it with faculties that had been trained in the
ways of Walter Scott Campbell, and then imparted it
by telephone to the magnate.

The famous Campbell chuckle rewarded the secretary several times. The idea that the son of his wife's
quondam schoolmate was shaking the foundations of
Kernville to bring the inhabitants to a realization of
the high condescension of the Walter Scott Campbells
in visiting their city with resulting benefits to the firm
of Ward & Ward, tickled Walter Scott enormously.

"Very good, Parker! Come back at your convenience. Subscribe for the local papers in your name.
We don't want to overlook anything!"

VII

The Campbells' visit was still ten days distant when
John, rising in the Sycamore Circuit Court to ask for
an injunction against certain persons who were removing gravel from the pits of a company that had lately
carried its business to Ward & Ward, was interrupted
by the bailiff who handed him a telegram.

"If your honor please——?" said John, bowing def-
erentially toward the person of the court.

The judge nodded, not a little impressed as the young attorney tore open the envelope and scanned the message, which read:

Have recommended your firm to certain corporations in which I am interested to counsel them in legal and business matters affecting your city. Please feel no compulsion to accept their commissions if not wholly agreeable to you.   W. S. CAMPBELL.

John thrust the message carelessly into his trousers' pocket, straightened his shoulders and proceeded with a terse explanation of the injury inflicted upon his client and the grounds upon which he sought the immediate relief of a restraining order.

The order was granted and in the midst of a parley over the amount of bond to be given by the petitioner the bailiff delivered into John's hands three more telegrams, one from the Sutphen Loan & Trust Company, another from The Ironsides Steel Casting Company, another from the general manager of the Transcontinental Lines west of Buffalo.

The message of the Sutphen Loan & Trust Company stated that it was sending an engineer to examine the plant of the Sycamore Water Power Company and would appreciate such confidential assistance as Ward & Ward might give him as to the personnel of the corporation. One of the vice-presidents of the steel casting company wished to make an appointment with Ward & Ward at the earliest date possible, letter of explanation to follow; matter strictly confidential. The Transcontinental official would reach Kernville shortly to take up the matter of certain improvements, and wished a conservative estimate of the local needs uninfluenced by the Chamber of Commerce or owners of property that might be needed in extensions. Matter confidential; letter to follow; please wire answer.

Ward, senior, with law books overflowing upon the floor from his desk, heard John's report of his success in protecting the gravel pits, read the telegrams, and asked hoarsely:

"Are we crazy, John, or has the whole world gone mad?"

"Nothing of the kind! We've been discovered; that's all! Campbell's a man of discernment, and he's spotted us as the solidest and most trustworthy citizens and lawyers of the Sycamore valley. Though all these messages are addressed to me, it's the brains of the firm he's recommending and that's you. I'm only the field man and business getter."

"You certainly get the business, son! Not counting anything we may get out of those people Campbell's sending us, we've got at least twenty-five thousand dollars' worth of business on the books right now!"

"Don't look so scared, dad! We're handling it all right. Within a week I've turned down four divorce cases and a breach of promise suit with love letters I'd rejoice to read to a farmer jury! Pick and choose; that's our motto! Where are the papers in Shipton *versus* Hovey. I'm getting a settlement there that will save Hovey about ten thousand bucks, and I want to tell him about it when I go up to see Alice tonight. I'll now wire our thanks to Campbell and date up these people he's sending to see us. Those wise guys that run the Chamber of Commerce are going to be frantic when they find the hope of a bigger Kernville lies right here in our office."

VIII

"I never expected a simple tea would cause so much trouble!" exclaimed Mrs. Ward at the dinner table five days before the day set for the Campbell visit. "I've simply got to send out the cards tomorrow!"

"Let me see that list again," said John. "It's first rate as it stands. You've put in all our new clients and that's the main thing. But if Mrs. Shepherd is to pour chocolate, you'll have to affix Mrs. Hovey to the tea pot to prevent hard feeling. I've got everything all set with Townley to make a big spread of Helen's engagement to Ned and mine to Alice next Sunday."

"Please don't be too noisy about it," pleaded Helen. "Since you began boosting the family I'm ashamed to look at the papers."

"Circulation of both sheets has gone up, sis. Everybody in the Sycamore valley's on tip-toe for news of the Wards and Campbells. Tomorrow the *Journal* will print exclusive information from our office that the mighty Ironsides corporation is to build a plant here. The happy word that the railroad yards are to be doubled and the shops enlarged will come from headquarters, but father will be interviewed to make sure we get the credit."

"I think I understand everything," said Helen gazing musingly at the engagement ring of which she had been the happy possessor for just twenty-four hours, "except how Mr. Campbell began sending those important people to you and father. You might almost think it was a joke of some kind."

"The joke certainly isn't on us! I've decided to turn down the nomination for prosecutor. As things are going I'd be a fool to sacrifice my private practice for a public job. The general counsel of the Transcontinental's feeling us out as to whether we'll take the local attorneyship of that rascally corporation. Canby Taylor's had it for twenty years, and it would be some triumph to add it to our string of scalps."

The invitation list, rigidly revised and cut to one hundred, was finally acceptable to all the members of the family, and Helen and John had begun to address the envelopes when this task was interrupted by the delivery of a telegram.

"It's for you, mother," said Helen, taking the envelope from the capped and aproned housemaid who had been installed in the household against the coming of the Campbells.

Mrs. Ward adjusted her glasses and settled herself to read with the resigned air of one inured to the idea that telegrams are solely a medium for communicating bad news.

"What is it, mother? Somebody dead?" asked John without looking up from the envelope he was addressing to The Hon. and Mrs. Addison Swiggert.

"Worse!" murmured Mrs. Ward, staring vacantly.

"Nothing can be worse!" ejaculated Helen, catching the bit of paper as it fell fluttering to the floor. "The Campbells are not coming!" she gasped.

"Not coming!" faltered Robert Fleming Ward, throwing down a brief he was studying.

"Read it, for heaven's sake!" commanded John.

Helen, with difficulty bringing her eyes to meet the dark tidings, began to read:

> So sorry we are obliged to change our plans and cannot pay you the visit to which we had looked forward with so much pleasure——

"It's horrible! It's positively tragic," sobbed Mrs. Ward, groping for her handkerchief.

"Hurry on, Helen!" ordered John. "There's a lot more of it."

> Walter feels that he ought to attend a conference of Southern bankers unexpectedly called for February eighteen at Baltimore, and we are obliged to defer the California trip indefinitely. However, we are going down in the yacht and Walter has happily solved the whole problem by insisting that you all come to New York and make the cruise with us.

"Glory! glory hallelujah!" John shouted.

> The yacht is big enough to be comfortable for even a poor sailor like me, so we can have a cosy time together. We want your busband, son and daughter to come of course, and you will be our guests throughout the journey. The Manager of the Transcontinental will put his private car at your disposal. Do wire at once that you will come. With much love.
>
> RUTH CAMPBELL.

"Can you beat it! *Can* you beat it!" cried John.

"After all this talk—and the publicity and everything——" his mother began plaintively.

"And all these people who've brought us business in the hope of meeting the Campbells and getting favors from him!" his father added hopelessly.

"My dear parents!" cried John pleadingly, flinging up his arm with a dramatic gesture he had found effective in commanding the attention of juries,—"my *dear* parents, nothing could be more fortunate! If the Campbells had come we'd have been hard put to please all these people who want the joy of shaking

big money by the hand. The old boy very shrewdly
switched all these business matters to father and me
to handle so we've already got about everything Kernville needs, and we've done it in a way that makes us
the best advertised law firm in the state."

"But the humiliation——" his mother began in a
hoarse whisper.

"Humiliation nothing!" John caught her up. "Don't
you realize that an announcement that the Campbells
are sending a private car to haul us down to their
yacht will make the biggest hit of all! And you're
going, mother—and you, Helen; and father's got to
go, too! You all deserve it, and I'll stay right here
and bask in the warm radiance of your grandeur while
the *White Gull* rides the waves."

"You think, then, the change won't ruin *everything?*"
his mother asked with a gulp.

"John's perfectly right!" [declared Helen. "The
Campbell name has already worked magic in our lives
and through us done wonders for Kernville. It will
be glorious to sail in a yacht! They didn't need to
ask us, and nothing could be friendlier or more cordial
than that telegram."

"That's true," Mr. Ward assented. "But I can't
possibly leave right now. There's that Lindley coal
case coming up for trial next week, and John's not
familiar with it."

"Yes, my dear father, but when you ask for a post-
ponement on the perfectly legitimate ground that
Walter Scott Campbell wants you to go yachting with
him, that case will be set forward and you will acquire
much merit in the eyes of the court! You'll need a
couple of white flannel suits and some rubber-soled
shoes, but you can pick them up in New York. Really

this change of plans is the biggest thing of all.   Take
this pad, mother, and write your acceptance, carefully
expressing my deep regret that owing to pressure of
professional duties I am unable to leave."

The announcement that Mr. and Mrs. Walter Scott
Campbell had been obliged to postpone their visit to
Mr. and Mrs. Robert Fleming Ward until spring,
but that Mr. and Mrs. Ward and Miss Helen were
to cruise with them in the *White Gull* did not fail of
the impression which John had predicted such a revela-
tion would make upon his fellow citizens.   A yacht
that would sail the winter seas was a challenge to the
imagination of home-keeping folk whose most daring
adventure upon the deep was an occasional cruise
in an excursion steamer on the Great Lakes.
Kernville was proud of the Wards, and so many citizens of both genders expressed their affection with
flowers that the car in which the trio set out for New
York looked like a bridal bower.
Ned Shepherd and Alice Hovey were at the station
with John to see them off and several hundred other
citizens looked on with mingled emotions of admiration
and envy.   The *Journal's* photographer caught an
excellent picture of Mrs. Ward and Helen, their arms
full of roses, standing on the rear platform as the train
pulled out.

"That boy of yours," remarked Walter Scott Campbell, as he sat with Robert Fleming Ward in the smoking
room of the *White Gull* as the yacht felt her way cautiously up Chesapeake Bay,—"That boy must be a
good deal of a lad.   Even at long range you can feel his
energy and enterprise."

"He's a good boy," Ward agreed diffidently, "and full of ginger. I get out of breath trying to keep up with him."

Campbell chuckled. "Knows a chance when he sees it." Another Campbell chuckle. "I like young-sters of that type. He's profited of course by your own long experience in the law?"

"He's as good a lawyer as I am now—more resource-ful, and a better hand in dealing with people."

"That boy knows more than the law," declared Campbell with another chuckle. "He knows human nature!"

As their eyes met Ward's face broke into a smile as he realized that Campbell understood everything, and was not at all displeased at the outrageous fashion in which John had used his name.

"You know of Gaspard & Collins, in New York?" asked the magnate. "They do a good deal of my legal work. They're looking for a young man, westerner preferred, to go into the firm, and it just occurs to me that your John would just suit them. I can understand how you would feel about losing him, but it's a good opportunity to get in touch with important affairs. Talk it over with your wife, and if you think well of the idea you can wire him tomorrow. It's a fair night; let's go on deck and watch the lights."

ARABELLA'S HOUSE PARTY

I

FARRINGTON read the note three times, fished the discarded envelope out of his wastepaper basket, scrutinized it thoroughly, and then addressed himself again to the neat vertical script. What he read was this:

> If Mr. Farrington will appear at the Sorona Tea House, on the Bayfield Road, near Corydon, at four o'clock today—Tuesday—the matter referred to in his reply to our advertisement may be discussed. We serve only one client at a time and our consultations are all strictly confidential.

The note was unsigned, and the paper, the taste and quality of which were beyond criticism, bore no address, The envelope had not passed through the post-office. but had been thrust by a private messenger into the R. F. D. box at Farrington's gate.

Laurance Farrington had been established in the Berkshires for a year, and his house in the hills back of Corydon, with the Housatonic tumbling through his meadow, had been much described in newspapers and literary journals as the ideal home for a bachelor author. He had remodeled an old farmhouse to conform to his ideas of comfort, and incidentally he maintained a riding horse, a touring car and a runabout; and he had lately set up an Airedale kennel.

He was commonly spoken of as one of the most successful and prosperous of American novelists. He not only satisfied the popular taste but he was on cordial terms with the critics. He was thirty-one, and since the publication of The Fate of Catherine Gaylord, in his twenty-fourth year, he had produced five other novels and a score or more of short stories of originality and power.

An enviable man was Laurance Farrington. When he went back to college for commencement he shared attention with presidents and ex-presidents; and governors of states were not cheered more lustily. He was considered a very eligible young man and he had not lacked opportunities to marry. His friends marveled that, with all his writing of love and marriage, he had never, so far as any one knew, been in love or anywhere near it.

As Farrington read his note in the quiet of his study on this particular morning it was evident that his good fortune had not brought him happiness. For the first time he was finding it difficult to write. He had begun a novel that he believed would prove to be the best thing he had done; but for three months he had been staring at blank paper. The plot he had relied on proved, the moment he began to fit its parts together, to be absurdly weak; and his characters had deteriorated into feeble, spineless creatures over whom he had no control. It was inconceivable that the mechanism of the imagination would suddenly cease to work, or that the gift of expression would pass from him without warning; and yet this had apparently happened.

Reading somewhere that Sir Walter Scott had found horseback riding stimulating to the imagination,

he galloped madly every afternoon, only to return tired
and idealess; and the invitations of his neighbors to
teas and dinners had been curtly refused or ignored.
It was then that he saw in a literary journal this
advertisement:

> PLOTS SUPPLIED. Authors in need of assis-
> tance served with discretion. Address X Y
> Z, care of office, *The Quill*.

To put himself in a class of amateurs requiring help
was absurd, but the advertisement piqued his curiosity.
Baker, the editor of The Quill, wrote him just then to
ask for an article on Tendencies in American Fiction;
and in declining this commission Farrington subjoined
a facetious inquiry as to the advertisement of X Y Z.
In replying, Baker said that copy for the ad had been
left at the business office by a stranger. A formal
note accompanying it stated that a messenger would
call later for answers.

"Of course," the editor added jocularly, "this is only
another scheme for extracting money from fledgling
inkslingers—the struggling geniuses of Peoria and
Ypsilanti. You're a lucky dog to be able to sit on
Olympus and look down at them."

Farrington forced his unwilling pen to its task for
another week, hoping to compel the stubborn fountains
to break loose with their old abundance. His critical
faculties were malevolently alert and keen, now that
his creative sense languished. He hated what he
wrote and cursed himself because he could do no better.

To add to his torture, the advertisement in The
Quill recurred to him persistently, until, in sheer frenzy,
he framed a note to X Y Z—an adroit feeler, which he
hoped would save his face in case the advertisement
had not been put forth in good faith.

Plots—he wrote—were the best thing he did; and as X Y Z seemed to be interested in the subject it might be amusing if not indeed profitable for them to meet and confer. This was the cheapest bravado; he had not had a decent idea of any sort for a year!

X Y Z was nothing if not prompt. The reply, naming the Sorona Tea House as a rendezvous, could hardly have reached him sooner; and the fact that it had been slipped into his mail box unofficially greatly stimulated his interest.

The Sorona Tea House stood on a hilltop two miles from Farrington's home and a mile from Corydon, his postoffice and center of supplies. It had been designed to lure motorists to the neighborhood in the hope of interesting them in the purchase of property. It was off the main thoroughfares and its prosperity had been meager; in fact, he vaguely remembered that some one had told him the Sorona was closed. But this was not important; if closed it would lend itself all the better to the purposes of the conference.

He lighted his pipe and tramped over his fields with his favorite Airedale until luncheon. It was good to be out-doors; good to be anywhere, in fact, but nailed to a desk. The brisk October air, coupled with the prospect of finding a solution of his problems before the day ended, brought him to a better mood, and he sat down to his luncheon with a good appetite.

When three o'clock arrived he had experienced a sharp reaction. He was sure he was making a mistake; he was tempted to pack a suit-case and go for a week-end with some friends on Long Island who had been teasing him for a visit; but this would not be a decent way to treat X Y Z, who might be making a long journey to reach the tea house.

The question of X Y Z's sex now became obtrusive.
Was the plot specialist man or woman? The hand-
writing in the note seemed feminine and yet it might
have been penned by a secretary. The use of *our* and
we rather pointed to more than one person. Very
likely this person who offered plots in so businesslike
a fashion was a spectacled professor who had gone
through all existing fiction, analyzing devices and making new combinations, and would prove an intolerable
bore—a crank probably; possibly an old maid who had
spent her life reading novels and was amusing herself
in her old age by furnishing novelists with ideas. He
smoked and pondered. He was persuaded that he
had made an ass of himself in answering the advertis,?-
ment and the sooner he was through with the business
the better.

He allowed himself an hour to walk to the Sorona,
and set off rapidly. He followed the road to the hilltop
and found the tea house undeniably there.

The place certainly had a forsaken look. The
veranda was littered with leaves, the doors and windows
were closed, and no one was in sight. Depression
settled on him as he noted the chairs and tables piled
high in readiness for storing for the winter. He
passed round to the western side of the house, and his
heart gave a thump as he beheld a table drawn close
to the veranda rail and set with a braver showing of
napery, crystal and silver than he recalled from his
few visits to the house in midsummer. A spirit lamp
was just bringing the kettle to the boiling point: it
puffed steam furiously. There were plates of sandwiches and cakes, cream and sugar, and cups—two cups!

"Good afternoon, Mr. Farrington! If you're quite
ready let's sit down."

He started, turned round and snatched off his hat.

A girl had appeared out of nowhere. She greeted him with a quick nod, as though she had known him always—as though theirs was the most usual and conventional of meetings. Then she walked to the table and surveyed it musingly.

"Oh, don't trouble," she said as he sprang forward to draw out her chair. "Let us be quite informal; and, besides, this is a business conference."

Nineteen, he guessed—twenty, perhaps; not a day more. She wore, well back from her face, with its brim turned up boyishly, an unadorned black velvet hat. Her hair was brown, and wisps of it had tumbled down about her ears; and her eyes—they, too, were brown—a golden brown which he had bestowed on his favorite heroine. They were meditative eyes—just such eyes as he might have expected to find in a girl who set up as a plot specialist. There was a dimple in her right cheek. When he had dimpled a girl in a story he bestowed dimples in pairs. Now he saw the superiority of the single dimple, which keeps the interested student's heart dancing as he waits for its appearance. Altogether she was a wholesome and satisfying young person, who sent scampering all his preconceived ideas of X Y Z.

"I'm so glad you were prompt! I always hate waiting for people," she said.

"I should always have hated myself if I had been late," he replied.

"A neat and courteous retort! You see the tea house is closed. That's why I chose it. Rather more fun anyhow, bringing your own things."

They were very nice things. He wondered how she had got them there.

"I hope," he remarked leadingly, "you didn't have to bring them far!"

She laughed merrily at his confusion as he realized that this was equivalent to asking her where she lived.

"Let's assume that the fairies set the table. Do you take yours strong?"

He delayed answering that she might poise the spoonful of tea over the pot as long as possible. Hers was an unusual hand; in his tales he had tried often to describe that particular hand without ever quite hitting it. He liked its brownness—tennis probably; possibly she did golf too. Whatever sports she affected, he was quite sure that she did them well.

"I knew you would like tea, for the people in your novels drink such quarts; and that was a bully short story of yours, The Lost Tea Basket—killingly funny—the real Farrington cleverness!"

He blinked, knowing how dead the real Farrington cleverness had become. Her manner was that of any well-brought-up girl at a tea table, and her attitude toward him continued to be that of an old acquaintance. She took him as a matter of course; and though this was pleasant, it shut the door on the thousand and one questions he wished to ask her.

Just now she was urging him to try the sandwiches; she had made them herself, she averred, and he need not be afraid of them.

"Perhaps," he suggested with an accession of courage, "you won't mind telling me your name."

"It was nice of you to come," she remarked dreamily, ignoring his question, "without asking for credentials. I'll be perfectly frank and tell you that I couldn't give you references if you asked for them; you're my first client! I almost said patient!" she added laughingly.

"If you had said patient you would have made no mistake! I've been out of sorts—my wits not working for months."

"I thought your last book sounded a little tired," she replied. "There were internal evidences of weariness. You rather worked the long arm of coincidence overtime, for example—none of your earlier bounce and zest. Even your last short story didn't quite get over—a little too self-conscious probably; and the heroine must have identified the hero the first time she saw him in his canoe."

She not only stated her criticisms frankly but she uttered them with assurance, as though she had every right to pass judgment on his performances. This was the least bit irritating. He was slightly annoyed—as annoyed as any man of decent manners dare be at the prettiest girl who has ever brightened his horizon. But this passed quickly.

Not only was she a pretty girl but he became conscious of little graces and gestures, and of a charming direct gaze, that fascinated him. And, for all her youth, she was very wise; he was confident of that.

"I must tell you that though I had dozens of letters, yours was the only one that appealed to me. A majority of them were frivolous, and some were from writers whose work I dislike. I had a feeling that if they were played out they never would be missed. But you were different; you are Farrington, and to have you fail would be a calamity to American literature."

He murmured his thanks. Her sympathetic tone was grateful to his bruised spirit. He had gone too far now to laugh away his appeal to her. And as the moments passed his reliance on her grew.

They talked of the weather, the hills and the autumn foliage, while he speculated as to her identity.

"Of course you know the Berkshires well, Miss——"

"A man who can't play a better approach than that certainly needs help!" she laughed.

He flushed and stammered.

"Of course I might have asked you directly if you lived in the Hills. But let us be reasonable. I'm at least entitled to your name; without that——"

"Without it you will be just as happy!"

"Oh, but you don't mean that you won't——"

"That's exactly what I mean!" She smiled, her elbows on the table, the slim brown fingers interlaced under her firm rounded chin.

"That isn't fair. You know me; and yet I'm utterly in the dark as to you——"

"Oh, names are not of the slightest importance. Of course X Y Z is rather awkward. Let's find another name—something you can call me by as a matter of convenience if, indeed, we meet again."

She bit into a macaroon dreamily while this took effect.

"Not meet again!" he exclaimed.

"Oh, of course it's possible we may not. We haven't discussed our business yet; but when we reach it you may not care for another interview."

"On a strictly social basis I can't imagine myself never seeing you again. As for my business, let it go hang!"

She lifted a finger with a mockery of warning.

"No business, no more tea; no more anything! You would hardly call the doctor or the lawyer merely to talk about the scenery. And by the same token you can hardly take the time of a person in my occupation without paying for it."

"But, Miss——"

"There you go again! Well, if you must have a name, call me Arabella! And never mind about 'Missing' me."

"You're the first Arabella I've ever known!" he exclaimed fervidly.

"Then be sure I'm the last!" she returned mockingly; then she laughed gayly. "Oh, rubbish! Let's be sensible. I have a feeling that the girls in your stories are painfully stiff, and they're a little too much alike. They're always just coming down from Newport or Bar Harbor, and we are introduced to them as they enter their marble palaces on Fifth Avenue and ring for Walters to serve tea at once. You ought to cut out those stately, impossible queens and go in for human interest. I'll be really brutal and say that I'm tired of having your heroine pale slightly as her lover—the one she sent to bring her an orchid known only to a cannibal tribe of the upper Amazon—appears suddenly at the door of her box at the Metropolitan, just as Wolfram strikes up his eulogy of love in Tannhauser. If one of the cannibals in his war dress should appear at the box door carrying the lover's head in a wicker basket, that would be interesting; but for Mister Lover to come wearing the orchid in his buttonhole is commonplace. Do you follow me?"

She saw that he flinched. No one had ever said such things to his face before.

"Oh, I know the critics praise you for your wonderful portrait gallery of women, but your girls don't strike me as being real spontaneous American girls. Do you forgive me?"

He would have forgiven her if she had told him she
had poisoned his tea and that he would be a dead man
in five minutes.

"Perhaps," he remarked boldly, "the fact that I
never saw you until to-day will explain my failures!"

"A little obvious!" she commented serenely.   "But
we'll overlook it this time.   You may smoke if you like."

She lighted a match for him and held it to the tip
of his cigarette. This brought him closer to the
brown eyes for an intoxicating instant.   Brief as that
moment was, he had detected on each side of her nose
little patches of freckles that were wholly invisible
across the table.   He was ashamed to have seen them,
but the knowledge of their presence made his heart
go pitapat.   His heart had always performed its physical functions with the utmost regularity, but as a
center of emotions he did not know it at all.   He must
have a care.   Arabella folded her hands on the edge of
the table.

"The question before us now is whether you wish to
advise with me as to plots. Before you answer you
will have to determine whether you can trust me.
It would be foolish for us to proceed if you don't think
I can help you.   On the other hand, I can't undertake
a commission unless you intrust your case to me fully.
And it wouldn't be fair for you to allow me to proceed
unless you mean to go through to the end. My
system is my own; I can't afford to divulge it unless
you're willing to confide in me."

She turned her gaze upon the gold and scarlet foliage
of the slope below, to leave him free to consider.   He
was surprised that he hesitated. As an excuse for
tea-table frivolity this meeting was well enough; as a
business proposition it was ridiculous.   But this

unaccountable Arabella appealed strongly to his imagination. If he allowed her to escape, if he told her he had answered the advertisement of X Y Z merely in jest, she was quite capable of telling him good-by and slipping away into the nowhere out of which she had come. No—he would not risk losing her; he would multiply opportunities for conferences that he might prolong the delight of seeing her.

"I have every confidence," he said in a moment, "that you can help me. I can tell you in a word the whole of my trouble."

"Very well, if you are quite sure of it," she replied.

"The plain truth about me is," he said earnestly —and the fear he had known for days showed now in his eyes——"the fact about me is that I'm a dead one! I've lost my stroke. To be concrete, I've broken down in the third chapter of a book I promised to deliver in January, and I can't drag it a line further!"

"It's as clear as daylight that you're in a blue funk," she remarked. "You're scared to death. And that will never do! You've got to brace up and cheer up! And the first thing I would suggest is——"

"Yes, yes!" he whispered eagerly.

"Burn those three chapters and every note you've made for the book."

"I've already burned them forty times!" he replied ruefully.

"Burn them again. Then in a week, say, if you follow my advice explicitly, it's quite likely you'll find a new story calling you."

"Just waiting won't do it! I've tried that."

"But not under my care," she reminded him with one of her enthralling smiles. "An eminent writer has declared that there are only nine basic plots known

to fiction; the rest are all variations. Let it be our
affair to find a new one—something that has never
been tried before!"

"If you could do that you'd save my reputation.
You'd pull me back from the yawning pit of failure!"

"Cease firing! You've been making hard work of
what ought to be the grandest fun in the world. The
Quill had a picture of you planted beside a beautiful
mahogany desk, waiting to be inspired. There's not
much in this inspiration business. You've got to choose
some real people, mix them up and let them go to
it!"

"But," Farrington frowned, "how are you ever
going to get them together? You can't pick out the
interesting people you meet in the street and ask them
to work up a plot for you."

"No," she asserted, "you don't ask them; you just
make them do it. You see"— taking up a cube of
sugar and touching it to the tip of her tongue—"every
living man and woman, old or young, is bitten with the
idea that he or she is made for adventure."

"Rocking-chair heroes," he retorted, "who'd cry
if they got their feet wet going home from church!"

"The tamer they are, the more they pine to hear
the silver trumpet of romance under their windows,"
she replied, her eyes dancing.

He was growing deeply interested. She was no
ordinary person, this girl.

"I see one obstacle," he replied dubiously. "Would
you mind telling me just how you're going to effect
these combinations—assemble the parts, so to speak;
or, in your more poetical manner, make the characters
harken to the silver horn?"

"That," she replied readily, "is the easiest part of

all! You've already lost so much time that this is an emergency case and we'll call them by telegraph!"

"You don't mean that—not really!"

"Just that! We'll have to decide what combination would be the most amusing. We should want to bring together the most utterly impossible people—people who'd just naturally hate each other if they were left in the same room. In that way you'd quicken the action."

He laughed aloud at the possibilities; but she went on blithely:

"We ought to have a person of national distinction —a statesman preferred; some one who figures a lot in the newspapers. Let's begin," she suggested, "with the person in all the United States who has the least sense of humor."

"The competition would be keen for that honor," said Farrington, "but I suggest the Honorable Tracy B. Banning, the solemnest of all the United States senators—Idaho or Rhode Island—I forget where he hails from. It doesn't matter."

"I hoped you'd think of him," she exclaimed, striking her hands together delightedly.

"He owns a house—huge, ugly thing—on the other side of Corydon."

"Um! I think I've heard of it," she replied indifferently.

She drew from her sweater pocket and spread on the table these articles: a tiny vanity box, a silver-backed memorandum book, two caramels and the stub of a lead-pencil. There was a monogram on the vanity box, and remembering this she returned it quickly to her pocket. He watched her write the Senator's name in her book, in the same vertical hand in which the note making the appointment had been written. She lifted her head, narrowing her eyes with the stress of thought.

"If a man has a wife we ought to include her, perhaps."

Farrington threw back his head and laughed.

"Seems to me his wife's divorcing him—or the other way round. The press has been featuring them lately."

"Representative of regrettable tendency in American life," she murmured. "They go down as Mr. and Mrs."

"Now it's your turn," he said.

"Suppose we put in a gay and cheerful character now to offset the Senator. I was reading the other day about the eccentric Miss Sallie Collingwood, of Portland, Maine; she's rich enough to own a fleet of yachts, but she cruises up and down the coast in a disreputable old schooner—has a mariner's license and smokes a pipe. Is she selected?"

"I can't believe there's anybody so worth while on earth!"

"That's your trouble!" she exclaimed, as she wrote the name. "Your characters never use the wrong fork for the fish course; they're all perfectly proper and stupid. Now it's your turn."

"It seems to me," he suggested, "that you ought to name all the others. As I think of it, I really don't know any interesting people. You're right about the tameness of my characters, and my notebooks are absolutely blank."

She merely nodded.

"Very well; I suppose it's only fair for me to supply the rest of the eggs for the omelet. Let me see; there's been a good deal in the papers about Birdie Coningsby, the son of the copper king, one of the richest young men in America. I've heard that he has red hair, and that will brighten the color scheme."

"Excellent!" murmured Farrington. "He was arrested last week for running over a traffic cop in New Jersey. I judge that the adventurous life appeals to him."

"I suppose our Senator represents the state; the church also should be represented. Why not a clergyman of some sort? A bishop rather appeals to me; why not that Bishop of Tuscarora who's been warning New York against its sinful ways?"

"All right. He's at least a man of courage; let's give him a chance."

"A detective always helps," Arabella observed meditatively.

"Then by all means put in Gadsby! I'm tired of reading of his exploits. I think he's the most conceited ass now before the public."

"Gadsby is enrolled!"

She held up the memorandum for his inspection.

"That's about enough to start things," she remarked. "It's a mistake to have too many characters in a novel. Of course others may be drawn in—we can count on that."

"But the heroine—a girl that realizes America's finest and best——"

"I think she should be the unknown quantity—left up in the air. But if you don't agree with that——"

"I was thinking," he said, meeting her eyes, "that possibly you——"

One of her most charming smiles rewarded this.

"As the chief plotter, I must stand on the side lines and keep out of it. But if you think——"

"I think," he declared, "that the plot would be a failure if you weren't in it—very much in it."

"Oh, we must pass that. But there might be a girl of some sort. What would you think of Zaliska?"

"The dancer! To offset the bishop!"

The mirth in her eyes kindled a quick response in his. She laughingly jotted down the name of the Servian dancer who had lately kicked her way into fame on Broadway.

"But do you think," he interposed, "that the call of the silver horn is likely to appeal to her? She'd need a jazz band!"

"Oh, variety is the spice of adventure! We'll give her a chance," she answered. "I think we have done well. One name more needs to be inscribed—that of Laurance Farrington."

She lifted her hand quickly as he demurred.

"You need experiences—adventures—to tone up your imagination. Perhaps Zaliska will be your fate; but there's always the unknown quantity."

They debated this at length. He insisted that he would be able to contribute nothing to the affair; that it was his lack of ideas which had caused him to appeal to her for help, and that it would be best for him to act the role of interested spectator.

"I'm sorry, but your objections don't impress me, Mr. Farrington. If you're not in the game you won't be able to watch it in all its details. So down you go!"

For a moment she pondered, with a wrinkling of her pretty brows, the memorandum before her; then she closed the book and dropped it into her sweater pocket. He was immensely interested in her next step, wondering whether she really meant to bring together the widely scattered and unrelated people she had selected for parts in the drama that was to be enacted for his benefit.

She rose so quickly that he was startled, gave a boyish tug at her hat—there was something rather boyish about her in spite of her girlishness—and said with an air of determination:

"How would Thursday strike you for the first rehearsal? Very well, then. There may be some difficulty in reaching all of them by telegraph; but that's my trouble. Just where to hold the meeting is a delicate question. We should have"—she bent her head for an instant—"an empty house with large grounds; somewhere in these hills there must be such a place. You know the country better than I. Maybe——"

"To give a house party without the owner's knowledge or consent is going pretty far; there might be legal complications," he suggested seriously.

"Timidity doesn't go in the adventurous life. And besides," she added calmly, "that matter doesn't concern us in the least. If they all get arrested it's so much the better for the plot. We can't hope for anything as grand as that!"

"But how about you! What if you should be discovered and go to jail! Imagine my feelings!"

"Oh, you're not to worry about me. That's my professional risk."

"Then, as to the place, what objection is there to choosing Senator Banning's house? He's in the cast anyhow. His place, I believe, hasn't been occupied for a couple of years. The gates were nailed up the last time I passed there."

She laughed at this suggestion rather more merrily than she had laughed before.

"That's a capital idea!   Particularly as we've chosen
him for his lack of humor!"

"If he has any fun in him he'll have a chance to
show it," said Farrington, "when he finds his house
filled with people he never saw before."

Questions of taste as to this procedure, hanging
hazily at the back of his consciousness, were dispelled
by Arabella's mirthful attitude toward the plan. He
could hardly tell this joyous young person that it would
be transcending the bounds of girlish naughtiness to
telegraph a lot of people she didn't know to meet at
the house of a gentleman who enjoyed national fame
for his lack of humor. Arabella would only laugh at
him. The delight that danced in her eyes was infectious
and the spirit of adventure possessed him. He was
impatient for the outcome: still, would she—dared she—
do it?

She had drawn on a pair of tan gloves and struck
her hands together lightly.

"This has been the nicest of little parties! I thank
you—the first of my clients!   But I must skip!"

He had been dreading the moment when she might
take it into her head to skip. They had lingered long
and the sun had dropped like a golden ball beyond the
woodland.

"But you will let me help with the tea things?" he
cried eagerly. "I can telephone from the crossroads
for my machine."

She ignored his offer. A dreamy look came into her
eyes.

"I wonder," she said with the air of a child proposing
a new game, "whether anyone's ever written a story
about a person—man or girl—who undertakes to find
some one; who seeks and seeks until it's a puzzling and

endless quest—and then finds that the quarry is himself
—or herself! Do you care for that? Think it over. I
throw that in merely as a sample. We can do a lot
better than that."

"Oh, you must put it in the bill!"

"Now," she said, "please, when you leave, don't
look back; and don't try to find me! In this business
who seeks shall never find. We place everything on the
knees of the gods. Thursday evening, at Mr. Banning's, at eight o'clock. Please be prompt."

Then she lifted her arms toward the sky and cried
out happily:

"There, sir, is the silver trumpet of romance! I
make you a present of it."

He raised his eyes to the faint outline of the new
moon that shone clearly through the tremulous dusk.

As he looked she placed her hands on the veranda
railing and vaulted over it so lightly that he did not
know she had gone until he heard her laughing as she
sprang away and darted through the shrubbery below.

From the instant Arabella disappeared Farrington
tortured himself with doubts. One hour he believed
in her implicitly; the next he was confident that she had
been playing with him and that he would never see her
again.

He rose early Wednesday morning and set out in
his runabout—a swift scouting machine—and covered
a large part of Western Massachusetts before nightfall.
Somewhere, he hoped, he might see her—this amazing
Arabella, who had handed him the moon and run away!
He visited the tea house; but every vestige of their
conference had been removed. He was even unable to
identify the particular table and chairs they had used.
He drove to the Banning place, looked at the padlocked

gates and the heavily shuttered windows, and hurried
on, torn again by doubts. He cruised slowly through
villages and past country clubs where girls adorned the
landscape, hoping for a glimpse of her. It was the
darkest day of his life, and when he crawled into bed
at midnight he was seriously questioning his own
sanity.

A storm fell on the hills in the night and the fateful
day dawned cold and wet. . He heard the rain on his
windows gratefully. If the girl had merely been making
sport of him he wanted the weather to do its worst. He
cared nothing for his reputation now; the writing of
novels was a puerile business, better left to women
anyhow. The receipt of three letters from editors asking for serial rights to his next book enraged him.
Idiots, not to know that he was out of the running
forever!

He dined early, fortified himself against the per-
sistent downpour by donning a corduroy suit and a
heavy mackintosh, and set off for the Banning place at
seven o'clock. Once on his way he was beset by a fear
that he might arrive too early. As he was to be a
spectator of the effects of the gathering, it would be
well not to be first on the scene. As he passed through
Corydon his engine changed its tune ominously and he
stopped at a garage to have it tinkered. This required
half an hour, but gave him an excuse for relieving his
nervousness by finishing the run at high speed.

A big touring car crowded close to him, and in response to fierce honkings he made way for it. His
headlights struck the muddy stern of the flying car and
hope rose in him. This was possibly one of the ad-
venturers hastening into the hills in response to Arabella's summons. A moment later a racing car, running

like an express train, shot by and his lamps played on
the back of the driver huddled over his wheel.

When he neared the Banning grounds Farrington
stopped his car, extinguished the lights and drove it in
close to the fence.

It was nearly eight-thirty and the danger of being
first had now passed. As he tramped along the muddy
road he heard, somewhere ahead, another car, evidently
seeking an entrance. Some earlier arrival had opened
the gates, and as he passed in and followed the curving
road he saw that the house was brilliantly lighted.

As he reached the steps that led up to the broad
main entrance he became panic-stricken at the thought
of entering a house the owner of which he did not know
from Adam, on an errand that he felt himself incapable
of explaining satisfactorily. He turned back and was
moving toward the gates when the short, burly figure
of a man loomed before him and heavy hands fell on
his shoulders.

"I beg your pardon!" said Farrington breathlessly.
An electric lamp flashed in his face, mud-splashed from
his drive, and his captor demanded his business. "I
was just passing," he faltered, "and I thought perhaps——"

"Well, if you thought perhaps, you can just come up
to the house and let us have a look at you," said the
stranger gruffly.

With a frantic effort Farrington wrenched himself
free; but as he started to run he was caught by the
collar of his raincoat and jerked back.

"None of that now! You climb right up to the house
with me. You try bolting again and I'll plug you."

To risk a bullet in the back was not to be considered
in any view of the matter, and Farrington set off with

as much dignity as he could assume, his collar tightly gripped by his captor.

As they crossed the veranda the front door was thrown open and a man appeared at the threshold. Behind him hovered two other persons.

"Well, Gadsby, what have you found?"

"I think," said Farrington's captor with elation, "that we've got the man we're looking for!"

Farrington was thrust roughly through the door and into a broad, brilliantly lighted hall.

II

Senator Banning was one of the most generously photographed of American statesmen, and the bewildered and chagrined Farrington was relieved to find his wits equal to identifying him from his newspaper pictures.

"Place your prisoner by the fireplace, where we can have a good look at him," the Senator ordered. "And, if you please, Gadsby, I will question him myself."

Rudely planted on the hearth, Farrington stared about him. Two of the persons on Arabella's list had answered the summons at any rate. His eyes ran over the others. A short, stout woman, wearing mannish clothes and an air of authority, advanced and scrutinized him closely.

"A very harmless person, I should say," she commented; and, having thus expressed herself sonorously, she sat down in the largest chair in the room.

The proceedings were arrested by a loud chugging and honking on the driveway.

Farrington forgot his own troubles now in the lively dialogue that followed the appearance on the scene of a handsome middle-aged woman, whose face betrayed surprise as she swept the room with a lorgnette for an instant, and then, beholding Banning, showed the keenest displeasure.

"I'd like to know," she demanded, "the precise meaning of this! If it's a trick—a scheme to compromise me—I'd have you know, Tracy Banning, that my opinion of you has not changed since I bade you farewell in Washington last April."

"Before we proceed farther," retorted Senator Banning testily, "I should like to ask just how you came to arrive here at this hour!"

She produced a telegram from her purse. "Do you deny that you sent that message, addressed to the Gassaway House at Putnam Springs? Do you suppose," she demanded as the Senator put on his glasses to read the message, "that I'd have made this journey just to see you?"

"Arabella suffering from nervous breakdown; meet me at Corydon house Thursday evening," read the Senator.

"Arabella ill!" exclaimed the indomitable stout lady. "She must have been seized very suddenly!"

"I haven't seen Arabella and I never sent you this telegram," declared the Senator. "I was brought here myself by a fraudulent message." He drew a telegram from his pocket and read impressively:

Arabella has eloped. Am in pursuit. Meet me at your house in Corydon Thursday evening. SALLIE COLLINGWOOD.

The stout lady's vigorous repudiation of this telegram consumed much time, but did not wholly appease the Senator. He irritably waved her aside, remarking sarcastically:

"It seems to me, Sallie Collingwood, that your presence here requires some explanation. I agreed to give
you the custody of Arabella while Frances and I were
settling our difficulties, because I thought you had wits
enough to take care of her. Now you appear to have
relinquished your charge, and without giving me any
notice whatever. I had supposed, even if you are my
wife's sister, that you would let no harm come to my
daughter."

"I'll trouble you, Tracy Banning, to be careful how
you speak to me!" Miss Collingwood replied. "Poor
Arabella was crushed by your outrageous behavior, and
if any harm has come to her it's your fault. She remained with me on the *Dashing Rover* for two weeks;
and last Saturday, when I anchored in Boston Harbor to
file proceedings against the captain of a passenger boat
who had foully tried to run me down off Cape Ann, she
ran away. Last night a telegram from her reached me
at Beverly saying you were effecting a reconciliation
and asking me to be here tonight to join in a family
jollification. Meantime I had wired to the Gadsby
Detective Agency to search for Arabella and asked them
to send a man here."

"Reconciliation," exploded the lady with the lorgnette, "has never been considered! And if I've been
brought here merely to be told that you have allowed
Arabella to walk off your silly schooner into the Atlantic
Ocean——"

"You may as well calm yourself, Frances. There's no
reason for believing that either Tracy or I had a thing
to do with this outrage."

"Well, Bishop Giddings is with me; he, too, has been
lured here by some one. We met on the train quite by
chance and I shall rely on his protection."

A black-bearded gentleman, who had followed Mrs. Banning into the hall and quietly peeled off a raincoat, was now disclosed in the garb of a clergyman—the Bishop of Tuscarora, Farrington assumed. He viewed the company quizzically, remarking:

"Well, we all seem to be having a good time!"

"A great outrage has been perpetrated on us," trumpeted the Senator. "I'm amazed to see you here, Bishop. Some lawless person has opened this house and telegraphed these people to come here. When I found Gadsby on the premises I sent him out to search the grounds; and I strongly suspect"—he deliberated and eyed Farrington savagely—"that the culprit has been apprehended."

A young man with fiery red hair, who had been nervously smoking a cigarette in the background, now made himself audible in a high piping voice:

"It's a sell of some kind, of course. And a jolly good one!"

This provoked an outburst of wrath from the whole company with the exception of Farrington, who leaned heavily on the mantel in a state of helpless bewilderment. These people seemed to be acquainted; not only were they acquainted but they appeared to be bitterly hostile to one another.

Mrs. Banning had wheeled on the red-haired young man, whom Farrington checked off Arabella's list as Birdie Coningsby, and was saying imperiously:

"Your presence adds nothing to my pleasure. If anything could increase the shame of my summons here you most adequately supply it."

"I'm sorry, Mrs. Banning," he pleaded; "but it's really not my fault. When Senator Banning telegraphed asking me to arrive here tonight for a weekend I assumed that it meant that Arabella——"

"Before we go further, Tracy Banning," interrupted the Senator's wife, "I want to be sure that your intimacy with this young scamp has ceased and that this is not one of your contemptible tricks to persuade me that he is a suitable man for my child to marry. After all the scandal we suffered on account of that landgrab you were mixed up in with old man Coningsby, I should think you'd stop trying to marry his son to my poor, dear Arabella!"

The Bishop of Tuscarora planted a chair behind Mrs. Banning just in time to save her from falling to the floor.

"Somebody has played a trick on all of us," said the detective. "My message was sent to my New York office and said that the Senator wished to see me here on urgent business. I got that message an hour after Miss Collingwood's and I have six men looking for the lost girl."

They compared notes with the result that each telegram was found to have been sent from a different railroad station between Great Barrington and Pittsfield. While this was in progress Farrington felt quite out of it and planned flight at the earliest moment. He pricked up his ears, however, as, with a loud laugh, the Bishop drew out his message and read it with oratorical effect:

Adventure waits! Hark to the silver bugle! Meet me at Tracy Banning's on Corydon Road via Great Barrington at eight o'clock Thursday evening.   X Y Z.

Farrington clung to the mantel for physical and

mental support. His mind was chaos; the Stygian Pit yawned at his feet. Beyond doubt, his Arabella of the tea table had dispatched messages to all the persons on her list; and, in the Bishop's case at least, she had given the telegram her own individual touch. No wonder they were paying no attention to him; the perspiration was trailing in visible rivulets down his mud-caked face and his appearance fully justified their suspicions.

"All my life," the Bishop of Tuscarora was explaining good-humoredly, "I have hoped that adventure would call me some day. When I got that telegram I heard the bugles blowing and set off at once. Perhaps if I hadn't known Senator Banning for many years, and hadn't married him when I was a young minister, I shouldn't have started for his house so gayly. Meeting Mrs. Banning on the train and seeing she was in great distress, I refrained from showing her my summons. How could I? But I'm in the same boat with the rest of you—I can't for the life of me guess why I'm here."

Farrington had been slowly backing toward a side door, with every intention of eliminating himself from the scene, when a heavy motor, which had entered the grounds with long, hideous honks, bumped into the entrance with a resounding bang, relieved by the pleasant tinkle of the smashed glass of its windshield.

Gadsby, supported by the agile Coningsby, leaped to the door; but before they could fortify it against attack it was flung open and a small, light figure landed in the middle of the room, and a young lady, a very slight, graceful young person in a modish automobile coat, stared at them a moment and then burst out laughing.

"Zaliska!" screamed Coningsby.

"Well," she cried, "that's what I call some entrance! Lordy! But I must be a sight!"

She calmly opened a violet leather vanity box, withdrew various trifles and made dexterous use of them, squinting at herself in a mirror the size of a silver dollar.

Farrington groaned and shuddered, but delayed his flight to watch the effect of this last arrival.

Banning turned on Coningsby and shouted:

"This is your work! You've brought this woman here! I hope you're satisfied with it!"

"My work!" piped Coningsby very earnestly in his queer falsetto. "I never had a thing to do with it; but if Zaliska is good enough for you to dine with in New York it isn't square for you to insult her here in your own house."

"I'm not insulting her. When I dined with her it was at your invitation, you little fool!" foamed the Senator.

Zaliska danced to him on her toes, planted her tiny figure before him and folded her arms.

"Be calm, Tracy; I will protect you!" she lisped sweetly.

"Tracy! Tracy!" repeated Mrs. Banning.

Miss Collingwood laughed aloud. She and the Bishop seemed to be the only persons present who were enjoying themselves. Outside, the machine that had brought Zaliska had backed noisily off the steps and was now retreating.

"Oh, cheer up, everybody!" said Zaliska, helping herself to a chair. "My machine's gone back to town; but I only brought a suit-case, so I can't stay forever.

By the way, you might bring it in, Harold," she remarked to Coningsby with a yawn.

Mrs. Banning alone seemed willing to cope with her.

"If you are as French as you look, mademoiselle, I suppose——"

"French, ha! Not to say aha! I sound like a toothpaste all right, but I was born in good old Urbana, Ohio. Your face registers sorrow and distress, madam. Kindly smile, if you please!"

"No impertinence, young woman! It may interest you to know that the courts haven't yet freed me of the ties that bind me to Tracy Banning, and until I get my decree he is still my husband. If that has entered into your frivolous head kindly tell me who invited you to this house."

The girl pouted, opened her vanity box, and slowly drew out a crumpled bit of yellow paper, which she extended toward her inquisitor with the tips of her fingers.

"This message," Mrs. Banning announced, "was sent from Berkville Tuesday night." And then her face paled. "Incredible!" she breathed heavily.

Gadsby caught the telegram as it fluttered from her hand.

"Read it!" commanded Miss Collingwood.

"MADEMOISELLE HELENE ZALISKA,
    New Rochelle, N. Y.
    Everything arranged. Meet me at Senator
    Banning's country home, Corydon, Massa-
    chusetts, Thursday evening at eight.
                    ALEMBERT GIDDINGS,
                        Bishop of Tuscarora."

The Bishop snatched the telegram from Gadsby

and verified the detective's reading with unfeigned astonishment. The reading of this message evoked another outburst of merriment from Miss Collingwood.

"Zaliska," fluted young Coningsby, "how dare you!"

"Oh, I never take a dare," said Zaliska. "I guessed it was one of your jokes; and I always thought it would be real sporty to be married by a bishop."

"Yes," said Miss Collingwood frigidly, "I suppose you've tried everything else!"

The Bishop met Mrs. Banning's demand that he explain himself with all the gravity his good-natured countenance could assume.

"It's too deep for me. I give it up!" he said. He crossed to Zaliska and took her hand.

"My dear young woman, I apologize as sincerely as though I were the guilty man. I never heard of you before in my life; and I wasn't anywhere near Berkville day before yesterday. The receipt of my own telegram in New Hampshire at approximately the same hour proves that irrefutably."

"Oh, that'll be all right, Bishop," said Zaliska. "I'm just as pleased as though you really sent it."

Miss Collingwood had lighted her pipe—a performance that drew from Zaliska an astonished:

"Well, did you ever! Gwendolin, what have we here?"

"What I'd like to know," cried Mrs. Banning, yielding suddenly to tears, "is what you've done with Arabella!"

The mention of Arabella precipitated a wild fusillade of questions and replies. She had been kidnapped, Mrs. Banning charged in tragic tones, and Tracy Banning should be brought to book for it.

"You knew the courts would give her to me and it was you who lured her away and hid her. This contemptible little Coningsby was your ideal of a husband for Arabella, to further your own schemes with his father. I knew it all the time! And you planned to meet him here, with this creature, in your own house! And he's admitted that you've been dining with her. It's too much! It's more than I should be asked to suffer, after all—after all—I've—borne!"

"Look here, Mrs. Lady; creature is a name I won't stand for!" flamed Zaliska.

"If you'll all stop making a rotten fuss——" wheezed Coningsby.

"If we can all be reasonable beings for a few minutes ——" began the Bishop.

Before they could finish their sentences Gadsby leaped to the doorway, through which Farrington was stealthily creeping, and dragged him back.

"It seems to me," said the detective, depositing Farrington, cowed and frightened, in the center of the group, which closed tightly about him, "that it's about time this bird was giving an account of himself. Everybody in the room was called here by a fake telegram, and I'm positive this is the scoundrel who sent 'em."

"He undoubtedly enticed us here for the purpose of robbery," said Senator Banning; "and the sooner we land him in jail the better."

"If you'll let me explain——" began Farrington, whose bedraggled appearance was little calculated to inspire confidence.

"We've already had too many explanations!" declared Mrs. Banning. "In all my visits to jails and penitentiaries I've rarely seen a man with a worse face than the prisoner's. I shouldn't be at all surprised if he turned out to be a murderer."

"Rubbish!" sniffed Miss Collingwood. "He looks like somebody's chauffeur who's been joy-rolling in the mud."

The truth would never be believed. Farrington resolved to lie boldly.

"I was on my way to Lenox and missed the road. I entered these grounds merely to make inquiries and get some gasoline. This man you call Gadsby assaulted me and dragged me in here; and, as I have nothing to do with any of you or your troubles, I protest against being detained longer."

Gadsby's derisive laugh expressed the general incredulity.

"You didn't say anything to me about gasoline! You were prowling round the house, and when I nabbed you you tried to bolt. I guess we'll just hold on to you until we find out who sent all those fake telegrams."

"We'll hold on to him until we find out who's kidnapped Arabella!" declared Mrs. Banning.

"That's a happy suggestion, Fanny," affirmed the Senator, for the first time relaxing his severity toward his wife.

"What's this outlaw's name?" demanded Miss Collingwood in lugubrious tones.

Clever criminals never disclosed their identity. Farrington had no intention of telling his name. He glowered at them as he involuntarily lifted his hand to his mud-spattered face. Senator Banning jumped back, stepping heavily on Coningsby's feet. Coningsby's howl of pain caused Zaliska to laugh with delight.

"If you hold me here you'll pay dearly for it," said Farrington fiercely.

"Dear, dear; the little boy's going to cry!" mocked the dancer. "I think he'd be nice if he had his face washed. By the way, who's giving this party anyhow? I'm perfectly famished and just a little teeny-teeny bite of food would go far toward saving your little Zaliska's life."

"That's another queer thing about all this!" exclaimed the Senator. "Some one has opened up the house and stocked it with provisions. The caretaker got a telegram purporting to be from me telling him I'd be down with a house party. However, the servants are not here. The scoundrel who arranged all this overlooked that."

This for some occult reason drew attention back to Farrington, and Gadsby shook him severely, presumably in the hope of jarring loose some information. Farrington resented being shaken. He stood glumly watching them and awaiting his fate.

"It looks as though you'd all have to spend the night here," remarked the Senator. "There are no trains out of Corydon until ten o'clock tomorrow. By morning we ought to be able to fix the responsibility for this dastardly outrage. In the meantime this criminal shall be locked up!"

"Shudders, and clank, clank, as the prisoner goes to his doom," mocked Zaliska.

"The sooner he's out of my sight the better," Mrs. Banning agreed heartily. "If he's hidden my poor dear Arabella away somewhere he'll pay the severest penalty of the law for it. I warn him of that."

"In some states they hang kidnappers," Miss Colling-

wood recalled, as though the thought of hanging gave
her pleasure.

"We'll put the prisoner in one of the servants' rooms
on the third floor," said the Senator; "and in the morning we'll drive him to Pittsfield and turn him over to
the authorities. Bring him along, Gadsby."

Gadsby dragged Farrington upstairs and to the back
of the house, with rather more force than was necessary.
Banning led the way, bearing a poker he had snatched
up from-the fireplace. Pushing him roughly into the
butler's room, Gadsby told Farrington to hold up his
hands.

"We'll just have a look at your pockets, young man.
No foolishness now!"

This was the last straw. Farrington fought. For
the first time in his life he struck a fellow man, and
enjoyed the sensation. He was angry, and the instant
Gadsby thrust a hand into his coat pocket he landed
on the detective's nose with all the power he could
put into the blow.

Banning dropped the poker and ran out, slamming
the door after him. Two more sharp punches in the
detective's face caused him to jump for a corner and
draw his gun. As he swung round, Farrington grabbed
the poker and dealt the officer's wrist a sharp thwack
that knocked the pistol to the floor with a bang. In a
second the gun was in Farrington's hand and he backed
to the door and jerked it open.

"Come in here, Senator!" he said as Banning's
white face appeared. "Don't yell or attempt to make
a row. I want you to put the key of that door on the
inside. If you don't I'm going to shoot your friend
here. I don't know who or what he is, but if you
don't obey orders I'm going to kill him. And if you're

not pretty lively with that key I'm going to shoot you too. Shooting is one of the best things I do—careful there, Mr. Gadsby! If you try to rush me you're a dead man!"

To demonstrate his prowess he played on both of them with the automatic. Gadsby stood blinking, apparently uncertain what to do. The key in Banning's hand beat a lively rat-tat in the lock as the frightened statesman shifted it to the inside. Farrington was enjoying himself; it was a sweeter pleasure than he had ever before tasted to find that he could point pistols and intimidate senators and detectives

"That will do; thanks! Now Mr. Gadsby, or whatever your name is, I must trouble you to remove yourself. In other words, get out of here—quick! There's a bed in this room and I'm going to make myself comfortable until morning. If you or any of you make any effort to annoy me during the night I'll shoot you, without the slightest compunction. And when you go downstairs you may save your faces by telling your friends that you've locked me up and searched me, and given me the third degree—and anything you please; but don't you dare come back! Just a moment more, please! You'd better give yourself first aid for nosebleed before you go down, Mr. Gadsby; but not here. The sight of blood is displeasing to me. That is all now. Good night, gentlemen!"

He turned the key, heard them conferring in low tones for a few minutes, and then they retreated down the hall. Zaliska had begun to thump the piano. Her voice rose stridently to the popular air: Any Time's A Good Time When Hearts are Light and Merry.

Farrington sat on the bed and consoled himself with a cigarette. As a fiction writer he had given much

study to human motives; but just why the delectable
Arabella had mixed him up in this fashion with the
company below was beyond him. Perversity was all
he could see in it. He recalled now that she herself
had chosen all the names for her list, with the exception
of Banning and Gadsby; and, now that he thought of
it, she had more or less directly suggested them.

To be sure he had suggested the Senator; but only in a
whimsical spirit, as he might have named any other
person whose name was familiar in contemporaneous
history. Arabella had accepted it, he remembered,
with alacrity. He had read in the newspapers about
the Bannings' marital difficulties, and he recalled that
Coningsby, a millionaire in one of the Western mining
states, had been implicated with Banning in a big irri-
gation scandal.

It was no wonder that Mrs. Banning had been out-
raged by her husband's efforts to marry Arabella to the
wheezing son of the magnate. In adding to the dramatis
personæ Zaliska, whose name had glittered on Broadway in the biggest sign that thoroughfare had ever seen,
Arabella had contributed another element to the situation which caused Farrington to grin broadly.

He looked at his watch. It was only nine-thirty,
though it seemed that eternity had rolled by since his
first encounter with Gadsby. He had taken a pistol
away from a detective of reputation and pointed it at a
United States Senator; and he was no longer the Farrington of yesterday, but a very different being, willing
that literature should go hang so long as he followed this
life of jaunty adventure.

After a brief rest he opened the door cautiously, crept
down the back stairs to the second floor, and, venturing
as close to the main stairway as he dared, heard lively

talk in the hall below. Gadsby, it seemed, was for leaving the house to bring help and the proposal was not meeting with favor.

"I refuse to be left here without police protection," Mrs. Banning was saying with determination. "We may all be murdered by that ruffian."

"He's undoubtedly a dangerous crook," said the officer; "but he's safe for the night. And in the morning we will take him to jail and find means of identifying him."

"Then for the love of Mike," chirruped Zaliska from the piano, "let's have something to eat!"

Farrington chuckled. Gadsby and Banning had not told the truth about their efforts to lock him up. They were both cowards, he reflected; and they had no immediate intention, at least, of returning to molest him. In a room where Banning's suitcase was spread open he acquired an electric lamp, which he thrust into his pocket. Sounds of merry activity from the kitchen indicated that Zaliska had begun her raid on the jam pots, assisted evidently by all the company.

One thought was uppermost in his mind—he must leave the house as quickly as possible and begin the search for Arabella. He wanted to look into her eyes again; he wanted to hear her laughter as he told of the result of her plotting. There was more to the plan she had outlined at the tea house than had appeared, and he meant to fathom the mystery; but he wanted to see her for her own sake. His pulses tingled as he thought of her—the incomparable girl with the golden-brown eyes and the heart of laughter!

He cautiously raised a window in one of the sleeping rooms and began flashing his lamp to determine his position. He was at the rear of the house and the rain

purred softly on the flat roof of a one-story extension of
the kitchen, fifteen feet below. The sooner he risked
breaking his neck and began the pursuit of Arabella
the better; so he threw out his rubber coat and let
himself out on the sill.

He dropped and gained the roof in safety. Below,
on one side, were the lights of the dining room, and
through the open windows he saw his late companions
gathered about the table. The popping of a cork
evoked cheers, which he attributed to Zaliska and
Coningsby. He noted the Bishop and Miss Collingwood in earnest conversation at one end of the room,
and caught a glimpse of Banning staggering in from
the pantry bearing a stack of plates, while his wife
distributed napkins. They were rallying nobly to
the demands upon their unwilling hospitality.

He crawled to the farther side of the roof, swung
over and let go, and the moment he touched the earth
was off with all speed for the road. It was good to be
free again, and he ran as he had not run since his
school-days, stumbling and falling over unseen obstacles in his haste. In a sunken garden he tumbled
over a stone bench with a force that knocked the wind
out of him; but he rubbed his bruised legs and resumed his flight.

Suddenly he heard some one running over the gravel
path that paralleled the driveway. He stopped to
listen, caught the glimmer of a light—the merest faint
spark, as of some one flashing an electric lamp—and
then heard sounds of rapid retreat toward the road.

Resolving to learn which member of the party was
leaving, he changed his course and, by keeping the
lights of the house at his back, quickly gained the
stone fence at the roadside.

When he had climbed halfway over he heard some one stirring outside the wall between him and the gate; then a motor started with a whir and an electric head-light was flashed on blindingly. As the machine pushed its way through the tangle of wet weeds into the open road he clambered over, snapped his lamp at the driver, and cried out in astonishment as the light struck Arabella full in the face.

She ducked her head quickly, swung her car into the middle of the road, and stopped.

"Who is that?" she demanded sharply.

"Wait just a minute! I want to speak to you; I have ten thousand things to say to you!" he shouted above the steady vibrations of the racing motor.

She leaned out, flashed her lamp on him, and laughed tauntingly. She was buttoned up tightly in a leather coat, but wore no hat; and her hair had tumbled loose and hung wet about her face. Her eyes danced with merriment.

"Oh, it's too soon!" she said, putting up her hand to shield her eyes from his lamp. "Not a word to say tonight; but tomorrow—at four o'clock—we shall meet and talk it over. You have done beauti-fully—superbly!" she continued. "I was looking through the window when they dragged you off up-stairs. And I heard every word everybody said! Isn't it perfectly glorious?—particularly Zaliska! What an awful mistake it would have been if we'd left her out! Back, sir! I'm on my way!"

Before he could speak, her car shot forward. He ran to his machine and flung himself into it; but Ara-bella was driving like a king's messenger. Her car, a low-hung gray roadster, moved with incredible speed. The rear light rose until it became a dim red star on the crest of a steep hill, and a second later it blinked him good-by as it dipped down on the farther side.

He gained the hilltop and let the machine run its maddest. When he reached the bottom he was sure he was gaining on the flying car, but suddenly the guiding light vanished. He checked his speed to study the trail more carefully, found that he had lost it, turned back to a crossroad where Arabella had plunged more deeply into the hills, and was off again.

The road was a strange one and hideously soggy. The tail light of Arabella's car brightened and faded with the varying fortunes of the two machines; but he made no appreciable gain. She was leading him into an utterly strange neighborhood, and after half a dozen turns he was lost.

Then his car landed suddenly on a sound piece of road and he stepped on the accelerator. The rain had ceased and patches of stars began to blink through the broken clouds, but as his hopes rose the light he was following disappeared; and a moment later he was clamping on the brakes.

The road had landed him at the edge of a watery waste, a fact of which he became aware only after he had tumbled out of his machine and walked off a dock. Some one yelled to him from a house at the water's edge and threatened to shoot if he didn't make himself scarce. And it was not Arabella's voice!

He slipped and fell on the wet planks, and his incidental remarks pertaining to this catastrophe were translated into a hostile declaration by the owner of the voice. A gun went off with a roar and Farrington sprinted for his machine.

"If you've finished your target practice," he called

from the car with an effort at irony, "maybe you'll tell what this place is!"

The reply staggered him:

"This pond's on Mr. Banning's place. It's private grounds and ye can't get through here. What ye doin' down here anyhow?"

Farrington knew what he was doing. He was looking for Arabella, who had apparently vanished into thin air; but the tone of the man did not encourage confidences. He was defeated and chagrined, to say nothing of being chilled to the bone.

"You orto turned off a mile back there; this is a private road," the man volunteered grudgingly, "and the gate ain't going to be opened no more tonight."

Farrington got his machine round with difficulty and started slowly back. His reflections were not pleasant ones. Arabella had been having sport with him. She had led him in a semicircle to a remote corner of her father's estate, merely, it seemed, that he might walk into a pond or be shot by the guardian of the marine front of the property.

He had not thought Arabella capable of such malevolence; it was not like the brown-eyed girl who had fed him tea and sandwiches two days before to lure him into such a trap. In his bewildered and depressed state of mind he again doubted Arabella.

He reached home at one o'clock and took counsel of his pipe until three, brooding over his adventure.

Hope returned with the morning. In the bright sunlight he was ashamed of himself for doubting Arabella; and yet he groped in the dark for an explanation of her conduct. His reasoning powers failed to find an explanation of that last trick of hers in leading him over the worst roads in Christendom, merely to drop him into a lake in her father's back yard.   She might have got rid of him easier than that!

The day's events began early.   As he stood in the doorway of his garage, waiting for the chauffeur to extract his runabout from its shell of mud, he saw Gadsby and two strange men flit by in a big limousine. As soon as his car was ready he jumped in and set off, with no purpose but to keep in motion.   He, the Farrington of cloistral habits, had tasted adventure; and it was possible that by ranging the county he might catch a glimpse of the bewildering Arabella, who had so disturbed the even order of his life.

He drove to Corydon, glanced into all the shops, and stopped at the post office on an imaginary errand. He bought a book of stamps and as he turned away from the window ran into the nautical Miss Collingwood.

"Beg pardon!" he mumbled, and was hurrying on when she took a step toward him.

"You needn't lie to me, young man; you were in that row at Banning's last night, and I want to know what you know about Arabella!"

This lady, who sailed a schooner for recreation, was less formidable by daylight.   It occurred to him that she might impart information if handled cautiously. They had the office to themselves and she drew him into a corner of the room and assumed an air of mystery.

"That fool detective is at the telegraph office wiring all the police in creation to look out for Arabella. You'd better not let him see you.   Gadsby is a brave man by daylight!"

"If Arabella didn't spend last night at her father's house I know nothing about her," said Farrington eagerly.   "I have reason to assume that she did."

She eyed him with frank distrust.

"Don't try to bluff me! You're mixed up in this row some way; and if you're not careful you'll spend the rest of your life in a large, uncomfortable penitentiary. If that man at the telegraph office wasn't such a fool——"

"You're not in earnest when you say Miss Banning wasn't at home last night!" he exclaimed.

"Decidedly I am! Do you suppose we'd all be chasing over the country this morning looking for my niece and offering rewards if we knew where she is? I live on a schooner to keep away from trouble, and this is what that girl has got me into! What's your name anyhow?"

He quickly decided against telling his name. At that moment Gadsby's burly frame became visible across Main Street, and Farrington shot out a side door and sprinted up an alley at his best speed. He struck the railroad track at a point beyond the station where it curved through the hills, and followed it for a mile before stopping to breathe.

As he approached a highway he heard a motor and flung himself down in the grass at the side of the track. The driver of the car checked its speed and one of his companions stood up and surveyed the long stretch of track. The blue glint of gun barrels caught Farrington's eye.

There were three men in the machine and he guiltily surmised that they were deputy sheriffs or constables looking for him. He stuck his nose into the ground and did not lift his head again until the sounds of the motor faded away in the distance. Probably no roads were safe, and even in following the railroad he might walk into an ambush.

He abandoned the ties for flight over a wooded hill.

It was hard going and the underbrush slapped him savagely in the face. A higher hill tempted him and a still higher one, and he came presently to the top of a young mountain. He sat for a time on a fallen tree and considered matters. In his perturbed state of mind it seemed to him that the faint clouds of dust he saw rising in the roads below were all evidences of pursuit. He picked out familiar landmarks and judged that his flight over the hills had brought him within four miles of his home.

Thoughts of home, and a tub, and clean clothes, pleased him, and he resolutely began the descent. The only way he could free himself from suspicion was by finding Arabella. And how could he find Arabella when he was likely at any moment to be run down by a country constable with a shotgun? And as for meeting Arabella at four o'clock, he realized now that he had stupidly allowed the girl to slip away from him without designating a meeting place.

So far as he knew, he was the only person who had seen Arabella since her escape from Miss Collingwood's schooner. It might be well for him to volunteer to the Bannings such information as he had; but the more he thought of this the less it appealed to him. It would be difficult to give a plausible account of his meeting with Arabella at the tea house; and, moreover, he shrank from a betrayal of the light-hearted follower of the silver trumpet. As a gentleman he could give no version of the affair that would not place all the blame on himself; and this involved serious risks.

He approached his house from the rear, keeping as far as possible from the road, lingered at the barn, dodged from it to the garage, and crept furtively into his study by a side door as the clock struck two.

He had seen none of his employees on the farm and the house was ominously still. He rang the bell and in a moment the scared face of Beeching was thrust in.

"Beg pardon; are you home, sir?" asked the servant with a frightened gulp.

"Of course I'm home!" said Farrington with all the dignity his scratched face and torn clothes would permit.

"I missed you, sir," said the man gravely. "I thought maybe you was off looking for Arabella."

The book Farrington had been nervously fingering fell with a bang.

"What—what the devil do you know about Arabella?"

"She's lost, sir. The kennel master and the chauffeur is off looking for her. It's a most singular case."

"Yes," Farrington assented; "most remarkable. Have there been any—er—have any people been looking here for—for her?"

"Well, sir, the sheriff stopped a while ago to ask whether we'd seen such a girl; and there was a constable on horseback, and citizens in machines. Her father has offered a reward of ten thousand dollars. And there's a man missing, they say, sir, a dangerous character they caught on the Banning place last night. There's a thousand on him; it's a kidnapping matter, sir."

Farrington's throat troubled him and he swallowed hard.

"It's a shameful case," he remarked weakly. "I hope they'll kill the rascal when they catch him."

"I hope so, sir," said Beeching. "You seem quite worn out, sir. Shall I serve something?"

"You may bring the Scotch—quick—and don't

bother about the water. And, Beeching, if anyone calls I'm out!"

By the time he had changed his clothes and eaten a belated luncheon it was three o'clock. From time to time mad honking on the highway announced the continuance of the search for Arabella. He had screwed his courage to the point of telephoning Senator Banning that Arabella had been seen near her father's place on the previous night. His spirits sank when the Corydon exchange announced that the Banning phone was out of order. The chauffeur, seeing Farrington's roadster on Main Street, telephoned from Corydon to know what disposition should be made of it, and Farrington ordered him to bring it home.

He regained his self-respect as he smoked a cigar. He had met the issues of the night and day bravely; and if further adventures lay before him he felt confident that he would acquit himself well. And, in spite of the tricks she had played on him, Arabella danced brightly in his thoughts. He must find Arabella!

He thrust the revolver he had captured from Gadsby into his pocket and drove resolutely toward the Bannings'.

A dozen machines blocked the entrance, indicating a considerable gathering, and he steeled himself for an interview that could hardly fail to prove a stormy one. The door stood open and a company of twenty people were crowded about a table. So great was their absorption that Farrington joined the outer circle without attracting attention.

"Mister Sheriff," Senator Banning was saying, "we shall make no progress in this affair until the man who escaped from custody here last night has been apprehended. You must impress a hundred—a thousand deputies into service if necessary, and begin a systematic search of every house, every hillside in Western Massachusetts. I suggest that you throw a line from here——"

They were craning their necks to follow his finger across the map spread out on the table, when Miss Collingwood's voice was heard:

"I tell you again I saw that man in the post office this morning, and the clerk told me he is Laurance Farrington, the fool who writes such preposterous novels."

"Madam," said the sheriff irritably, "you've said that before; but it's impossible! I know Mr. Farrington and he wouldn't harm a flea. And the folks at his house told me an hour ago that he was away looking for the lost girl."

"Only a bluff!" squeaked Coningsby. "He looked to me like a bad man."

"Oh, I didn't think he looked so rotten," said Zaliska; "but if he's Farrington I must say his books bore me to death!"

"Please remember this isn't a literary club!" shouted Senator Banning. "What do we care about his books if he's a kidnapper! What we're trying to do is to plan a thorough search of Berkshire County—of the whole United States, if necessary."

"So far as I'm concerned——" began Farrington in a loud voice; but as twenty other voices were raised at the same moment no one paid the slightest attention to him. Their indifference enraged him and he pushed his way roughly to the table and confronted Banning. "While you've wasted your time looking for me I've

been—— Stand back! Don't come a step nearer until
I've finished or I'll kill you!"

It was Gadsby who had caused the interruption, but
the whole room was now in an uproar. With every one
talking at once Coningsby's high voice alone rose above
the tempest. He wished he was armed; he would do
terrible things!

"Let the man tell his story," pleaded Mrs. Banning
between sobs.

"I've spent the night and day looking for Arabella!"
Farrington cried. "I have no other interest—no other
aim in life but to find Arabella. All I can tell you is
that I saw her at the Sorona Tea House Tuesday afternoon, and that last night she was on these grounds;
in fact, she saw you all gathered here and heard everything that was said in this room."

"Young man, you know too little or too much," said
Banning. "Gadsby, do your duty!"

The detective took a step forward, looked into the
barrel of his own automatic, and paused, waving his
hand to the sheriff and his deputies to guard the doors
and windows.

"How do you know she was at the tea house?" asked
Mrs. Banning. "It seems to me that's the first question."

"I met her there," Farrington blurted. "I met her
there by appointment!"

"Then you admit, you villian," began Banning,
choking with rage, "that you lured my daughter, an
innocent child, to a lonely tea house; that you saw her
last night; and that now—now!—you know nothing of
her whereabouts! This, sir, is——"

"Oh, it's really not so bad!" came in cheery tones
from above. "It was I who lured Mr. Farrington to the

tea house, and I did it because I knew he was a gentleman."

Farrington had seen her first—the much-sought Arabella—stealing down the stairway to the landing, where she paused and leaned over the railing, much at ease, to look at them.

Her name was spoken in gasps, in whispers, and was thundered aloud only by Miss Collingwood.

"This was my idea," said Arabella quietly as they all turned toward her. "I've been hiding in the old cottage by the pond, right here on father's place—with John and Mary, who've known me since I was a baby. This is my house party—a scheme to get you all together. I thought that maybe, if papa and mama really thought I was lost, and if papa and Mr. Coningsby and Mademoiselle Zaliska all met under the same roof, they might understand one another better—and me

"I telegraphed for Mr. Gadsby," she laughed, "just to be sure the rest of you were kept in order! And I sent for Bishop Giddings because he's an old friend, and I thought he might help to straighten things out."

She choked and the tears brightened her eyes as she stood gazing down at them.

"You needn't worry about me, Arabella," said Coningsby; "for Zaliska and I were married by the Bishop at Corydon this morning."

This seemed to interest no one in particular, though Miss Collingwood sniffed contemptuously.

Mrs. Banning had started toward Arabella, and at the same moment Senator Banning reached the stairway. Arabella tripped down three steps, then paused on tiptoe, with her hands outstretched, half-inviting, half-repelling them. She was dressed as at the tea house, but her youthfulness was lost for the moment in a grave wistfulness that touched Farrington deeply.

"You can't have me," she cried to her father and mother, "unless we're all going to be happy together again!"

.   .   .   .

Half an hour later Senator Banning and his wife, and Arabella, wreathed in smiles, emerged from the library and found the sheriff and his deputies gone; but the members of the original house party still lingered.

"Before I leave," said Gadsby, "I'd like to know just how Mr. Farrington got into the game. He refuses to tell how he came to see you at the tea house. I think we ought to know that."

"Oh," said Arabella, clapping her hands, "that's another part of the story. If Mr. Farrington doesn't mind——"

"Now that you're found I don't care what you tell," Farrington declared.

"You may regret that," said Arabella, coloring deeply. "I sat by Mr. Baker, of *The Quill*, at a dinner a little while ago, and we were talking about your books. And he said—he said your greatest weakness as a novelist was due to your never having—well"— she paused and drew closer under the protecting arm of her father—"you had never yourself been, as the saying is—in love— and he thought—— Well, this is shameful —but he and I—just as a joke—thought we d try to attract your attention by printing that plot advertisement. He said you were working too hard and seemed worried, and might bite; and then I thought it would be good fun to throw you into the lion's den here to stir things up, as you did. And I had my car on the road last night ready to skip if things got too warm. Of course I couldn't let you catch me; it would have spoiled all the fun! And it was I who shot off that gun last night to scare you—when old John was scolding you away from the place. But it was nasty of me, and not fair; and now, when everything else is all fixed and I'm so happy, I'm ashamed to look you in the face, knowing what a lot of trouble I've given you. And you'll always hate me——"

"I shall always love you," said Farrington, stepping forward boldly and taking her hands. "You've made me live for once in my life—you've made me almost human," he laughed. "And you've made me a braver man than I know how to be! You pulled down the silver trumpet out of heaven and gave it to me, and made me rich beyond words; and without you I should be sure to lose it again!"

THE THIRD MAN

I

WHEN Webster G. Burgess asked ten of his cronies to dine with him at the University Club on a night in January they assumed that the president of the White River National had been indulging in another adventure which he wished to tell them about.

In spite of their constant predictions that if he didn't stop hiding crooks in his house and playing tricks on the Police Department he would ultimately find himself in jail, Mr. Burgess continued to find amusement in frequent dallyings with gentlemen of the underworld. In a town of approximately three hundred thousand people a banker is expected to go to church on Sundays and otherwise conduct himself as a decent, orderly, and law-abiding citizen, but the president of the White River National did not see things in that light. As a member of the Board of Directors of the Released Prisoners' Aid Society he was always ready with the excuse that his heart was deeply moved by the misfortunes of those who keep to the dark side of the street, and that sincere philanthropy covered all his sins in their behalf.

When his friends met at the club and found Governor Eastman one of the dinner party, they resented the presence of that dignitary as likely to impose restraints upon Burgess, who, for all his jauntiness, was not wholly without discretion. But the governor was a good fellow,

as they all knew, and a story-teller of wide reputation.
Moreover, he was taking his job seriously, and, being
practical men, they liked this about him.   It was said
that no governor since Civil War times had spent so
many hours at his desk or had shown the same zeal
and capacity for gathering information at first hand
touching all departments of the State government.
Eastman, as the country knows, is an independent
character, and it was this quality, shown first as a prosecuting attorney, that had attracted attention and landed
him in the seat of the Hoosier governors.

"I suppose," remarked Kemp as they sat down,
"that these tablets are scattered around the table so
we can make notes of the clever things that will be
said here to-night.   It's a good idea and gives me a
chance to steal some of your stories, governor."

A scratch pad with pencil attached had been placed at
each plate, and the diners spent several minutes in
chaffing Burgess as to the purpose of this unusual table
decoration.

"I guess," said Goring, "that Web is going to ask us
to write limericks for a prize and that the governor
is here to judge the contest.   Indoor winter sports don't
appeal to me; I pass."

"I'm going to write notes to the House Committee on
mine," said Fanning; "the food in this club is not what
it used to be, and it's about time somebody kicked."

"As I've frequently told you," remarked Burgess,
smiling upon them from the head of the table, "you
fellows have no imagination.   You'd never guess what
those tablets are for, and maybe I'll never tell you."

"Nothing is so innocent as a piece of white paper,"
said the governor, eyeing his tablet.   "We'd better be
careful not to jot down anything that might fly up

and hit us afterward. For all we know, it may be a scheme to get our signatures for Burgess to stick on notes without relief from valuation or appraisement laws. It's about time for another Bohemian oats swindle, and our friend Burgess may expect to work us for the price of the dinner."

"Web's bound to go to jail some day," remarked Ramsay, the surgeon, "and he'd better do it while you're in office, governor. You may not know that he's hand in glove with all the criminals in the country: he quit poker so he could give all his time to playing with crooks."

"The warden of the penitentiary has warned me against him," replied the governor easily. "Burgess has a man at the gate to meet convicts as they emerge, and all the really bad ones are sent down here for Burgess to put up at this club."

"I never did that but once," Burgess protested, "and that was only because my mother-in-law was visiting me and I was afraid she wouldn't stand for a burglar as a fellow guest. My wife's got used to 'em. But the joke of putting that chap up here at the club isn't on me, but on Ramsay and Colton. They had luncheon with him one day and thanked me afterward for introducing them to so interesting a man. I told them he was a manufacturer from St. Louis, and they swallowed it whole. Pettit was the name, but he has a string of aliases as long as this table, and there's not a rogues' gallery in the country where he isn't indexed. You remember, Colton, he talked a good deal of his travels, and he could do so honestly, as he'd cracked safes all the way from Boston to Seattle."

Ramsay and Colton protested that this could not be so; that the man they had luncheon with was a shoe manufacturer and had talked of his business as only an expert could.

The governor and Burgess exchanged glances, and both laughed.

"He knew the shoe business all right enough," said Burgess, "for he learned it in the penitentiary and proved so efficient that they made him foreman of the shop!"

"I suppose," said Kemp, "that you've got another crook coming to take that vacant chair. You'd better tell us about him so we won't commit any social errors."

At the governor's right there was an empty place, and Burgess remarked carelessly that they were shy a man, but that he would turn up later.

"I've asked Tate, a banker at Lorinsburg, to join us and he'll be along after a while. Any of you know Tate? One of our scouts recently persuaded him to transfer his account to us, and as this is the first time he's been in town since the change I thought it only decent to show him some attention. We're both directors in a company that's trying to develop a tile factory in his town, so you needn't be afraid I'm going to put anything over on you. Tate's attending a meeting to-night from which I am regrettably absent! He promised to be here before we got down to the coffee."

As the dinner progressed the governor was encouraged to tell stories, and acceded good-naturedly by recounting some amusing things that had happened in the course of his official duties.

"But it isn't all so funny," he said gravely after keeping them in a roar for half an hour. "In a State as big as this a good many disagreeable things happen, and people come to me every day with heartbreaking stories. There's nothing that causes me more anxiety than the appeals for pardon; if the pardoning power were taken away from me, I'd be a much happier man. The Board of Pardons winnows out the cases, but even at that there's enough to keep me uncomfortable. It isn't the pleasantest feeling in the world that as you go to bed at night somebody may be suffering punishment unjustly, and that it's up to you to find it out. When a woman comes in backed by a child or two and cries all over your office about her husband who's doing time and tells you he wasn't guilty, it doesn't cheer you much; not by a jugful! Wives, mothers, and sisters: the wives shed more tears, the sisters put up the best argument, but the mothers give you more sleepless nights."

"If it were up to me," commented Burgess, "I'm afraid I'd turn 'em all out!"

"You would," chorused the table derisively, "and when you'd emptied the penitentiaries you'd burn 'em down!"

"Of course there's bound to be cases of flagrant injustice," suggested Kemp. "And the feelings of a man who is locked up for a crime he never committed must be horrible. We hear now and then of such cases and it always shakes my faith in the law."

"The law does the best it can," replied the governor a little defensively, "but, as you say, mistakes do occur. The old saying that murder will out is no good; we can all remember cases where the truth was never known. Mistakes occur constantly, and it's the fear of not rectifying them that's making a nervous wreck of me. I have in my pocket now a blank pardon that I meant to sign before I left my office, but I couldn't quite bring myself to the point. The Pardon Board has made the recommendation, not on the grounds of injustice—more,

I'm afraid, out of sympathy than anything else—and
we have to be careful of our sympathies in these matters.
And here again there's a wife to reckon with. She's
been at my office nearly every day for a year, and she's
gone to my wife repeatedly to enlist her support.
And it's largely through Mrs. Eastman's insistence that
I've spent many weeks studying the case. It's a
murder: what appeared to be a heartless, cold-blooded
assassination. And some of you may recall it—the
Avery case, seven years ago, in Salem County."

Half the men had never heard of it and the others
recalled it only vaguely.

"It was an interesting case," Burgess remarked,
wishing to draw the governor out. "George Avery was
a man of some importance down there and stood high
in the community. He owned a quarry almost eleven
miles from Torrenceville and maintained a bungalow
on the quarry land where he used to entertain his
friends with quail hunting and perhaps now and then
a poker party. He killed a man named Reynolds who
was his guest. As I remember, there seemed to be
no great mystery about it, and Avery's defense was a
mere disavowal and a brilliant flourish of character
witnesses."

"For all anybody ever knew, it was a plain case, as
Burgess says," the governor began. "Avery and
Reynolds were business acquaintances and Avery had
invited Reynolds down there to discuss the merging
of their quarry interests. Reynolds was found dead
a little way from the bungalow by some of the quarry
laborers. He had been beaten on the head, with a club
in the most barbarous fashion. Reynolds's overcoat
was torn off and the buttons ripped from his waistcoat,
pointing to a fierce struggle before his assailant got

him down and pounded the life out of him. The purpose was clearly not robbery, as Reynolds had a considerable sum of money on his person that was left untouched. When the men who found the body went to rouse Avery he collapsed when told that Reynolds was dead. In fact, he lay in a stupor for a week, and they could get nothing out of him. Tracks? No; it was a cold December night and the ground was frozen.

"Reynolds had meant to take a midnight train for Chicago, and Avery had wired for special orders to stop at the quarry station, to save Reynolds the trouble of driving into Torrenceville. One might have supposed that Avery would accompany his visitor to the station, particularly as it was not a regular stop for night trains and the way across the fields was a little rough. I've personally been over all the ground. There are many difficult and inexplicable things about the case, the absence of motive being one of them. The State asserted business jealousy and substantiated it to a certain extent, and the fact that Avery had taken the initiative in the matter of combining their quarry interests and might have used undue pressure on Reynolds to force him to the deal is to be considered."

The governor lapsed into silence, seemingly lost in reverie. With his right hand he was scribbling idly on the tablet that lay by his plate. The others, having settled themselves comfortably in their chairs, hoping to hear more of the murder, were disappointed when he ceased speaking. Burgess's usual calm, assured air deserted him. He seemed unwontedly restless, and they saw him glance furtively at his watch.

"Please, governor, won't you go on with the story?" pleaded Colton. "You know that nothing that's said at one of Web's parties ever goes out of the room."

"That," laughed the governor, "is probably unfortunate, as most of his stories ought to go to the grand jury. But if I may talk here into the private ear of you gentlemen I will go on a little further. I've got to make up my mind in the next hour or two about this case, and it may help me to reach a conclusion to think aloud about it."

"You needn't be afraid of us," said Burgess encouragingly. "We've been meeting here—about the same crowd—once a month for five years, and nobody has ever blabbed anything."

"All right; we'll go a bit further. Avery's stubborn silence was a contributing factor in his prompt conviction. A college graduate, a high-strung, nervous man, hard-working and tremendously ambitious; successful, reasonably prosperous, happy in his marriage, and with every reason for living straight: there you have George Avery as I make him out to have been when this calamity befell him. There was just one lapse, one error, in his life, but that didn't figure in the case, and I won't speak of it now. His conduct from the moment of his arrest, a week following the murder, and only after every other possible clue had been exhausted by the local authorities, was that of a man mutely resigned to his fate. I find from the records that he remained at the bungalow in care of a physician, utterly dazed, it seemed, by the thing he had done, until a warrant was issued and he was put in jail. He's been a prisoner ever since, and his silence has been unbroken to this day. His wife assures me that he never, not even to her, said one word about the case more than to declare his innocence. I've seen him at the penitentiary on two occasions, but could get nothing out of him.

In fact, I exhausted any ingenuity I may have in attempting to surprise him into some admission that would give me ground for pardoning him, but without learning anything that was not in the State's case. They're using him as a bookkeeper, and he's made a fine record: a model convict. The long confinement has told seriously on his health, which is the burden of his wife's plea for his release, but he wouldn't even discuss that.

"There was no one else at the bungalow on the night of the murder," the governor continued. "It was Avery's habit to get his meals at the house of the quarry superintendent, about five hundred yards away, and the superintendent's wife cared for the bungalow, but the men I've had at work couldn't find anything in that to hang a clue on. You see, gentlemen, after seven years it's not easy to work up a case, but two expert detectives that I employed privately to make some investigations along lines I suggested have been of great assistance. Failing to catch the scent where the trial started, I set them to work backward from a point utterly remote from the scene. It was a guess, and ordinarily it would have failed, but in this case it has brought results that are all but convincing."

The tablets and pencils that had been distributed along the table had not been neglected. The guests, without exception, had been drawing or scribbling; Colton had amused himself by sketching the governor's profile. Burgess seemed not to be giving his undivided attention to the governor's review of the case. He continued to fidget, and his eyes swept the table with veiled amusement. Then he tapped a bell and a waiter appeared.

"Pardon me a moment, governor, till the cigars are passed again."

In his round with the cigar tray the Jap, evidently by prearrangement, collected the tablets and laid them in front of Burgess.

"Changed your mind about the Limerick contest, Web?" asked some one.

"Not at all," said Burgess carelessly; "the tablets have fulfilled their purpose. It was only a silly idea of mine anyhow." They noticed, however, that a tablet was left at the still vacant place that awaited the belated guest, and they wondered at this, surmising that Burgess had planned the dinner carefully and that the governor's discussion of the Avery case was by connivance with their host. With a quickening of interest they drew their chairs closer to the table.

"The prosecuting attorney who represented the State in the trial is now a judge of the Circuit Court," the governor resumed when the door closed upon the waiter. "I have had many talks with him about this case. He confesses that there are things about it that still puzzle him. The evidence was purely circumstantial, as I have already indicated; but circumstantial evidence, as Thoreau once remarked, may be very convincing, as when you find a trout in the milk! But when two men have spent a day together in the house of one of them, and the other is found dead in a lonely place not far away, and suspicion attaches to no one but the survivor—not even the tramp who usually figures in such speculations—a jury of twelve farmers may be pardoned for taking the State's view of the matter."

"The motive you spoke of, business jealousy, doesn't seem quite adequate unless it could be established that they had quarreled and that there was a clear showing of enmity," suggested Fullerton, the lawyer.

"You are quite right, and the man who prosecuted Avery admits it," the governor answered.

"There may have been a third man in the affair," suggested Ramsey, "and I suppose the cynical must have suggested the usual woman in the case."

"I dare say those possibilities were thrashed out at the time," the governor replied; "but the only woman in this case is Avery's wife, and she and Reynolds had never met. I have found nothing to sustain any suspicion that there was a woman in the case. Avery's ostensible purpose in asking Reynolds to visit him at that out-of-the-way place was merely that they could discuss the combination of their quarry interests privately, and close to Avery's plant. It seems that Avery had undertaken the organization of a big company to take over a number of quarries whose product was similar, and that he wished to confer secretly with Reynolds to secure his sanction to a selling agreement before the others he wanted to get into the combination heard of it. That, of course, is perfectly plausible; I could make a good argument justifying that. Reynolds, like many small capitalists in country towns, had a number of irons in the fire and had done some promoting on his own hook. All the financial genius and all the financial crookedness aren't confined to Wall Street, though I forget that sometimes when I'm on the stump! I'm disposed to think from what I've learned of both of them that Avery wasn't likely to put anything over on Reynolds, who was no child in business matters. And there was nothing to show that Avery had got him down there for any other

purpose than to effect a merger of quarry interests for
their mutual benefit."

"There probably were papers to substantiate that,"
suggested Fullerton; "correspondence and that sort
of thing."

"Certainly; I have gone into that," the governor
replied. "All the papers remain in the office of the
prosecuting attorney, and I have examined them carefully. Now, if Avery had been able to throw suspicion
on some one else you'd think he'd have done so. And
if there had been a third person at the bungalow that
night you'd imagine that Avery would have said so;
it's not in human nature for one man to take the blame
for another's crime, and yet we do hear of such things,
and I have read novels and seen plays built upon that
idea. But here is Avery with fifteen years more to
serve, and, if he's been bearing the burden and suffering
the penalty of another's sin, I must say that he's taking
it all in an amazing spirit of self-sacrifice."

"Of course," said Fullerton, "Reynolds may have had
an enemy who followed him there and lay in wait for
him. Or Avery may have connived at the crime without being really the assailant. That is conceivable."

"We'll change the subject for a moment," said the
governor, "and return to our muttons later."

He spoke in a low tone to Burgess, who looked at
his watch and answered audibly:

"We have half an hour more."

The governor nodded and, with a whimsical smile,
began turning over the tablets.

"These pads were placed before you for a purpose
which I will now explain. I apologize for taking advantage of you, but you will pardon me, I'm sure, when
I tell you my reason. I've dipped into psychology

lately with a view to learning something of the mind's eccentricities. We all do things constantly without conscious effort, as you know; we perform acts automatically without the slightest idea that we are doing them. At meetings of our State boards I've noticed that nobody ever uses the pads that are always provided except to scribble on. Many people have that habit of scribbling on anything that's handy. Hotel keepers knowing this, provide pads of paper ostensibly for memoranda that guests may want to make while at the telephone, but really to keep them from defacing the wall. Left alone with pencil and paper, most of us will scribble something or draw meaningless figures.

"Sometimes it's indicative of a deliberate turn of mind; again it's sheer nervousness. After I had discussed this with a well-known psychologist I began watching myself and found that I made a succession of figure eights looped together in a certain way—I've been doing it here!

"And now," he went on with a chuckle, "you gentlemen have been indulging this same propensity as you listened to me. I find on one pad the word Napoleon written twenty times with a lot of flourishes; another has traced a dozen profiles of a man with a bulbous nose: it is the same gentleman, I find, who honored me by drawing me with a triple chin—for which I thank him. And here's what looks like a dog kennel repeated down the sheet. Still another has sketched the American flag all over the page. If the patriotic gentleman who drew the flag will make himself known, I should like to ask him whether he's conscious of having done that before?"

"I'm guilty, governor," Fullerton responded. "I believe it is a habit of mine. I've caught myself doing it scores of times."

"I'm responsible for the man with the fat nose," confessed Colton; "I've been drawing him for years without ever improving my draftsmanship."

"That will do," said the governor, glancing at the door. "We won't take time to speak of the others, though you may be relieved to know that I haven't got any evidence against you. Burgess, please get these works of art out of the room. We'll go back to the Avery case. In going over the papers I found that the prosecuting attorney in his search of the bungalow the morning after the murder found a number of pieces of paper that bore an odd, irregular sort of sketch. I'm going to pass one of them round, but please send it back to me immediately."

He produced a sheet of letter paper that bore traces of hasty crumpling, but it had been smoothed out again, and held it up. It bore the lithographed name of the Avery Quarry Company. On it was drawn this device:

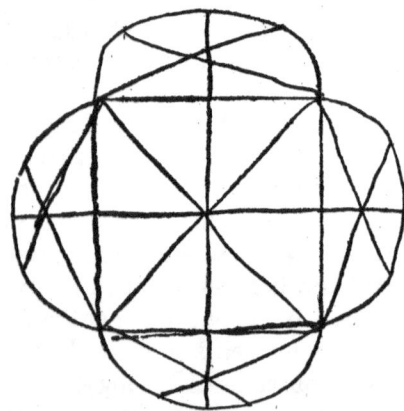

"Please note," said the governor as the paper passed from hand to hand, "that that same device is traced there five times, sometimes more irregularly than others, but the general form is the same. Now, in the fireplace of the bungalow living room they found this and three other sheets of the same stationery that bore this same figure. It seems a fair assumption that some one sitting at a table had amused himself by sketching these outlines and then, when he had filled the sheet, tore it off and threw it into the fireplace, wholly unconscious of what he was doing. The prosecutor attached no importance to these sheets, and it was only by chance that they were stuck away in the file box with the other documents in the case."

"Then you suspect that there was a third man in the bungalow that night?" Ramsay asked.

The governor nodded gravely.

"Yes; I have some little proof of it, quite a bit of proof, in fact. I have even had the wastebasket of the suspect examined for a considerable period. Knowing Burgess's interest in such matters, I have been using him to get me certain information I very much wanted. And our friend is a very successful person! I wanted to see the man I have in mind and study him a little when he was off-guard, and Burgess has arranged that for me, though he had to go into the tile business to do it! As you can readily see, I could hardly drag him to my office, so this little party was gotten up to give me a chance to look him over at leisure."

"Tate!" exclaimed several of the men.

"You can see that this is a very delicate matter," said the governor slowly. "Burgess thought it better not to have a smaller party, as Tate, whom I never saw, might think it a frame-up. So you see we are using you as stool-pigeons, so to speak. Burgess vouches for you as men of discretion and tact; and it will be your business to keep Tate amused and his attention away from me while I observe him a little."

"And when I give the signal you're to go into the library and look at picture books," Burgess added.

"That's not fair!" said Fullerton. "We want to see the end of it!"

"I'm so nervous," said Colton, "I'm likely to scream at any minute!"

"Don't do it!" Burgess admonished. "The new House Committee is very touchy about noise in the private dining rooms, and besides I've got a lot of scenery set for the rest of the evening, and I don't want you fellows to spoil it."

"It begins to look," remarked the governor, glancing at his watch, "as though some of our scenery might have got lost."

"He'd hardly bolt," Burgess replied; "he knows of no reason why he should! I told the doorman to send him right up. When he comes there will be no more references to the Avery case: you all understand?"

They murmured their acquiescence, and a solemn hush fell upon them as they turned involuntarily toward the vacant chair.

"This will never do!" exclaimed the governor, who seemed to be the one tranquil person in the room. "We must be telling stories and giving an imitation of weary business men having a jolly time. But I'm tired of talking; some of the good story-tellers ought to be stirred up."

With a little prodding Fullerton took the lead, but was able to win only grudging laughter. Colton was trying his hand at diverting them when they were startled by a knock. Burgess was at the door instantly and flung it open.

II

"Ah, Tate! Come right in; the party hasn't started yet!"

The newcomer was a short, thickset man, clean shaven, with coarse dark hair streaked with gray. The hand he gave the men in succession as they gathered about him for Burgess's introduction was broad and heavy. He offered it limply, with an air of embarrassment.

"Governor Eastman, Mr. Tate; that's your seat by the governor, Tate," said Burgess. "We were just listening to some old stories from some of these fellows, so you haven't missed anything. I hope they didn't need me at that tile meeting; I never attend night meetings: they spoil my sleep, which my doctor says I've got to have."

"Night meetings," said the governor, "always give me a grouch the next morning. A party like this doesn't, of course!'

"Up in the country where I live we still stick to lodge meetings as an excuse when we want a night off," Tate remarked.

They laughed more loudly than was necessary to put him at ease. He refused Burgess's offer of food and drink and when some one started a political discussion they conspired to draw him into it. He was County Chairman of the party not then in power and complained good-naturedly to the governor of the big plurality Eastman had rolled up in the last election. He talked slowly, with a kind of dogged emphasis, and it was evident that politics was a subject to his taste. His brown eyes, they were noting, were curiously large and full, with a bilious tinge in the white. He met a glance steadily, with, indeed, an almost disconcerting directness.

Where the governor sat became, by imperceptible degrees, the head of the table as he began seriously and frankly discussing the points of difference between the existing parties, accompanied by clean-cut characterizations of the great leaders.

There was nothing to indicate that anything lay behind his talk; to all appearances his auditors were absorbed in what he was saying. Tate had accepted a cigar, which he did not light but kept twisting slowly in his thick fingers.

"We Democrats have had to change our minds about a good many things," the governor was saying. "Of course we're not going back to Jefferson" (he smiled broadly and waited for them to praise his magnanimity in approaching so near to an impious admission), "but the world has spun around a good many times since Jefferson's day. What I think we Democrats do and do splendidly is to keep close to the changing current of public opinion; sometimes it seems likely to wash us down, as in the free-silver days; but we give, probably without always realizing it, a chance for the people to express themselves on new questions, and if we've stood for some foolish policies at times the country's the better for having passed on them. These great contests clear the air like a storm, and we all go peacefully about our business afterward."

As he continued they were all covertly watching Tate, who dropped his cigar and began playing with the pencil before him, absently winding and unwinding it upon the string that held it to the tablet. They were feigning an absorption in the governor's recital which their quick, nervous glances at Tate's hand belied. Burgess had pushed back his chair to face the governor more comfortably and was tying knots in his napkin.

Now and then Tate nodded solemnly in affirmation of something the governor said, but without lifting his eyes from the pencil. His broad shoulders were bent over the table, and the men about him were reflecting that this was probably an attitude into which his heavy body often relaxed when he was pondering deeply.

Wearying of the pencil—a trifle of the dance-card variety—he dropped it and drew his own from his waistcoat pocket. Then, after looking up to join in a laugh at some indictment of Republicanism expressed in droll terms by the governor, he drew the tablet closer and, turning his head slightly to one side, drew a straight line. Burgess frowned as several men changed position the better to watch him. The silence deepened, and the governor's voice rose with a slight oratorical ring. Through a half-open window floated the click of billiard balls in the room below. The governor having come down to the Wilson Administration, went back to Cleveland, whom he praised as a great leader and a great president. In normal circumstances there would have been interruptions and questions and an occasional jibe; and ordinarily the governor, who was not noted for loquacity, would not have talked twenty minutes at a stretch without giving an opportunity to his companions to break in upon him. He was talking, as they all knew, to give Tate time to draw the odd device which it was his habit to sketch when deeply engrossed.

The pencil continued to move over the paper; and from time to time Tate turned the pad and scrutinized his work critically. The men immediately about him watched his hand, wide-eyed, fascinated. There was something uncanny and unreal in the situation: it was like watching a wild animal approaching a trap and wholly unmindful of its danger. The square box which formed the base of the device was traced clearly; the arcs which were its familiar embellishment were carefully added. The governor, having exhausted Cleveland, went back to Jackson, and Tate finished a second drawing, absorbed in his work and rarely lifting his eyes.

Seeing that Tate had tired of this pastime, the governor brought his lecture to an end, exclaiming:

"Great Scott, Burgess! Why haven't you stopped me! I've said enough here to ruin me with my party, and you hadn't the grace to shut me off."

"I'm glad for one," said Tate, pushing back the pad, "that I got in in time to hear you; I've never known before that any Democrat could be so broad-minded!"

"The governor loosens up a good deal between campaigns," said Burgess, rising. "And now, let's go into the library where the chairs are easier."

The governor rose with the others, but remained by his chair, talking to Tate, until the room cleared, and then resumed his seat.

"This is perfectly comfortable; let's stay here, Mr. Tate. Burgess, close the door, will you."

Tate hesitated, looked at his watch, and glanced at Burgess, who sat down as though wishing to humor the governor, and lighted a cigar.

"Mr. Tate," said the governor unhurriedly, "if I'm not mistaken, you are George Avery's brother-in-law."

Tate turned quickly, and his eyes widened in surprise.

"Yes," he answered in slow, even tones; "Avery married my sister."

"Mr. Tate, I have in my pocket a pardon all ready to sign, giving Avery his liberty. His case has troubled me a good deal; I don't want to sign this pardon unless I'm reasonably sure of Avery's innocence. If you were in my place, Mr. Tate, would you sign it?"

The color went out of the man's face and his jaw fell; but he recovered himself quickly.

"Of course, governor, it would be a relief to me, to my sister, all of us, if you could see your way to pardoning George. As you know, I've been doing what I could to bring pressure to bear on the Board of Pardons: everything that seemed proper. Of course," he went on ingratiatingly, "we've all felt the disgrace of the thing."

"Mr. Tate," the governor interrupted, "I have reason to believe that there was a third man at Avery's bungalow the night Reynolds was killed. I've been at some pains to satisfy myself of that. Did that ever occur to you as a possibility?"

"I suspected that all along," Tate answered, drawing his handkerchief slowly across his face. "I never could believe George Avery guilty; he wasn't that kind of man!"

"I don't think he was myself," the governor replied. "Now, Mr. Tate, on the night of the murder you were not at home, nor on the next day when your sister called you on the long-distance telephone. You were in Louisville, were you not?"

"Yes, certainly; I was in Louisville."

"As a matter of fact, Mr. Tate, you were not in Louisville! You were at Avery's bungalow that night, and you left the quarry station on a freight train that was sidetracked on the quarry switch to allow the Chicago train to pass. You rode to Davos, which you reached at two o'clock in the morning. There you registered under a false name at the Gerber House, and went home the next evening pretending to have been at Louisville. You are a bachelor, and live in rooms over your bank, and there was no one to keep tab on your absences but your clerks, who naturally thought nothing of your going to Louisville, where business often takes you. You were there two days ago, I believe. But that has nothing to do with this matter. When you heard that Reynolds was dead and Avery under suspicion you answered your sister's summons and hurried to Torrenceville."

"I was in Louisville; I was in Louisville, I tell you!" Tate uttered the words in convulsive gasps. He brushed the perspiration from his forehead impatiently and half rose.

"Please sit down, Mr. Tate. You had had trouble a little while before that with Reynolds about some stock in a creamery concern in your county that he promoted. You thought he had tricked you, and very possibly he had. The creamery business had resulted in a bitter hostility between you: it had gone to such an extent that he had refused to see you again to discuss the matter. You brooded over that until you were not quite sane where Reynolds was concerned: I'll give you the benefit of that. You asked your brother-in-law to tell you when Reynolds was going to see him, and he obligingly consented. We will assume that Avery, a good fellow and anxious to aid you, made a meeting possible. Reynolds wasn't to know that you were to be at the bungalow—he wouldn't have gone if he had known it—and Avery risked the success of his own negotiations by introducing you into his house, out of sheer good will and friendship. You sat at a table in the bungalow living-room and discussed the matter. Some of these things only I have guessed at; the rest of it——"

"It's a lie; it's all a damned lie! This was a scheme to get me here: you and Burgess have set this up on me! I tell you I wasn't at the quarry; I never saw Reynolds there that night or any other time. My God, if I had been there,—if Avery could have put it on me, would he be doing time for it?"

"Not necessarily, Mr. Tate. Let us go back a little. It had been in your power once to do Avery a great favor, a very great favor. That's true, isn't it?"

Tate stared, clearly surprised, but his quivering lips framed no answer.

"You had known him from boyhood, and shortly after his marriage to your sister it had been in your power to do him a great favor; you had helped him out of a hole and saved the quarry for him. It cost me considerable money to find that out, Mr. Tate, and not a word of help have I had from Avery: be sure of that! He had been guilty of something just a little irregular— in fact, the forging of your name to a note—and you had dealt generously with him, out of your old-time friendship, we will say, or to spare your sister humiliation."

"George was in a corner," said Tate weakly but with manifest relief at the turn of the talk. "He squared it all long ago."

"It's natural, in fact, instinctive, for a man to protect himself, to exhaust all the possibilities of defense when the law lays it hand upon him. Avery did not do so, and his meek submission counted heavily against him. But let us consider that a little. You and Reynolds left the bungalow together, probably after the interview had added to your wrath against him, but you wished to renew the talk out of Avery's hearing and volunteered to guide Reynolds to the station where the Chicago train was to stop for him. You didn't go back, Mr. Tate——"

"Good God, I tell you I wasn't there! I can prove that I was in Louisville; I tell you——"

"We're coming back to your alibi in a moment," said the governor patiently. "We will assume— merely assume for the moment—that you said you would take the train with Reynolds and ride as far as Ashton, where the Midland crosses and you would get an early morning train home. Avery went to sleep at the bungalow wholly ignorant of what had happened; he was awakened in the morning with news that Reynolds had been killed by blows on the head inflicted near the big derrick where you and Reynolds—I am assuming again—had stopped to argue your grievances. Avery—shocked, dazed, not comprehending his danger and lying there in the bungalow prostrated and half-crazed by the horror of the thing—waited: waited for the prompt help he expected from the only living person who knew that he had not left the bungalow. He knew you only as a kind, helpful friend, and I dare say at first he never suspected you! It was the last thing in the world he would have attributed to you, and the possibility of it was slow to enter his anxious, perturbed mind. He had every reason for sitting tight in those first hideous hours, confident that the third man at that bungalow gathering would come forward and establish his innocence with a word. As is the way in such cases, efforts were made to fix guilt upon others; but Avery, your friend, the man you had saved once, in a fine spirit of magnanimity, waited for you to say the word that would clear him. But you never said that word, Mr. Tate. You took advantage of his silence; a silence due, we will say, to shock and horror at the catastrophe and to his reluctance to believe you guilty of so monstrous a crime or capable of allowing him, an innocent man, to suffer the penalty for it."

Tate's big eyes were bent dully upon the governor. He averted his gaze slowly and reached for a glass of water, but his hand shook so that he could not lift it, and he glared at it as though it were a hateful thing.

"I wasn't there! Why——" he began with an effort at bravado; but the words choked him and he sat swinging his head from side to side and breathing heavily.

The governor went on in the same low, even tone he had used from the beginning:

"When Avery came to himself and you still were silent, he doubtless saw that, having arranged for you to meet Reynolds at the bungalow—Reynolds, who had been avoiding you—he had put himself in the position of an accessory before the fact and that even if he told the truth about your being there he would only be drawing you into the net without wholly freeing himself. At best it was an ugly business, and being an intelligent man he knew it. I gather that you are a secretive man by nature; the people who know you well in your own town say that of you. No one knew that you had gone there and the burden of the whole thing was upon Avery. And your tracks were so completely hidden: you had been at such pains to sneak down there to take advantage of the chance Avery made for you to see Reynolds and have it out with him about the creamery business, that suspicion never attached to you. You knew Avery as a good fellow, a little weak, perhaps, as you learned from that forgery of your name ten years earlier; and it would have been his word against yours. I'll say to you, Mr. Tate, that I've lain awake at nights thinking about this case, and I know of nothing more pitiful, my imagination can conjure nothing more horrible, than the silent suffering of George Avery as he waited for you to go to his rescue, knowing that you alone could save him."

"I didn't do it, I didn't do it!" Tate reiterated in a hoarse whisper that died away with a queer guttural sound in his throat.

"And now about your alibi, Mr. Tate; the alibi that you were never even called on to establish," the governor reached for the tablet and held it before the man's eyes, which focused upon it slowly, uncomprehendingly. "Now," said the governor, "you can hardly deny that you drew that sketch, for I saw you do it with my own eyes. I'm going to ask you, Mr. Tate, whether this drawing isn't also your work?"

He drew out the sheet of paper he had shown the others earlier in the evening and placed it beside the tablet. Tate jumped to his feet, staring wild-eyed, and a groan escaped him. The governor caught his arm and pushed him back into his chair.

"You will see that that is Avery's letter-head that was used in the quarry office. As you talked there with Reynolds that night you played with a pencil as you did here a little while ago and without realizing it you were creating evidence against yourself that was all I needed to convince me absolutely of your guilt. I have three other sheets of Avery's paper bearing the same figure that you drew that night at the quarry office; and I have others collected in your own office within a week! As you may be aware, the power of habit is very strong. For years, no doubt, your sub-consciousness has carried that device, and in moments

of deep abstraction with wholly unrelated things your
hand has traced it.   Even the irregularities in the outline are identical, and the size and shading are precisely
the same.   I ask you again, Mr. Tate, shall I sign the
pardon I brought here in my pocket and free George
Avery?"

The sweat dripped from Tate's forehead and trickled
down his cheeks in little streams that shone in the light.
His collar had wilted at the fold, and he ran his finger
round his neck to loosen it.   Once, twice, he lifted his
head defiantly, but, meeting the governor's eyes fixed
upon him relentlessly, his gaze wavered.   He thrust
his hand under his coat and drew out his pencil and
then, finding it in his fingers, flung it away, and his
shoulders drooped lower.

III

Burgess stood by the window with his back to them.
The governor spoke to him, and he nodded and left the
room.   In a moment he returned with two men and
closed the door quickly.

"Hello, warden; sit down a moment, will you?"

The governor turned to a tall, slender man whose
intense pallor was heightened by the brightness of his
oddly staring blue eyes.   He advanced slowly.   His
manner was that of a blind man moving cautiously in
an unfamiliar room.   The governor smiled reassuringly
into his white, impassive face.

"I'm very glad to see you, Mr. Avery," he said.
He rose and took Avery by the hand.

At the name Tate's head went up with a jerk.   His
chair creaked discordantly as he turned, looked up into
the masklike face behind him, and then the breath went

out of him with a sharp, whistling sound as when a man dies, and he lunged forward with his arms flung out upon the table.

The governor's grip tightened upon Avery's hand; there was something of awe in his tone when he spoke.

"You needn't be afraid, Avery," he said. "My way of doing this is a little hard, I know, but it seemed the only way. I want you to tell me," he went on slowly, "whether Tate was at the bungalow the night Reynolds was killed. He *was* there, wasn't he?"

Avery wavered, steadied himself with an effort, and slowly shook his head. The governor repeated his question in a tone so low that Burgess and the warden, waiting at the window, barely heard. A third time he asked the question. Avery's mouth opened, but he only wet his lips with a quick, nervous movement of the tongue, and his eyes met the governor's unseeingly.

The governor turned from him slowly, and his left hand fell upon Tate's shoulder.

"If you are not guilty, Tate, now is the time for you to speak. I want you to say so before Avery; that's what I've brought him here for. I don't want to make a mistake. If you say you believe Avery to be guilty, I will not sign his pardon."

He waited, watching Tate's hands as they opened and shut weakly; they seemed, as they lay inert upon the table, to be utterly dissociated from him, the hands of an automaton whose mechanism worked imperfectly. A sob, deep, hoarse, pitiful, shook his burly form.

The governor sat down, took a bundle of papers from his pocket, slipped one from under the rubber band which snapped back sharply into place. He drew out a pen, tested the point carefully, then, steadying it with his left hand, wrote his name.

"Warden," he said, waving the paper to dry the ink; "thank you for your trouble. You will have to go home alone. Avery is free."

IV

When Burgess appeared at the bank at ten o'clock the next morning he found his friends of the night before established in the directors' room waiting for him. They greeted him without their usual chaff, and he merely nodded to all comprehendingly and seated himself on the table.

"We don't want to bother you, Web," said Colton, "but I guess we'd all feel better if we knew what happened after we left you last night. I hope you don't mind."

Burgess frowned and shook his head.

"You ought to thank God you didn't have to see the rest of it! I've got a reservation on the Limited to night: going down to the big city in the hope of getting it out of my mind."

"Well, we know only what the papers printed this morning," said Ramsay; "a very brief paragraph saying that Avery had been pardoned. The papers don't tell the story of his crime as they usually do, and we noticed that they refrained from saying that the pardon was signed at one of your dinner parties."

"I fixed the newspapers at the governor's request. He didn't want any row made about it, and neither did I, for that matter. Avery is at my house. His wife was there waiting for him when I took him home."

"We rather expected that," said Colton, "as we were planted at the library windows when you left the club. But about the other man: that's what's troubling us."

"Um," said Burgess, crossing his legs and clasping his knees. "*That* was the particular hell of it."

"Tate was guilty; we assume that of course," suggested Fullerton. "We all saw him signing his death warrant right there at the table."

"Yes," Burgess replied gravely, "and he virtually admitted it; but if God lets me live I hope never to see anything like that again!"

He jumped down and took a turn across the room.

"And now—— After that, Web?"

"Well, it won't take long to tell it. After the governor signed the pardon I told the warden to take Avery downstairs and get him a drink: the poor devil was all in. And then Tate came to, blubbering like the vile coward he is, and began pleading for mercy: on his knees, mind you; on his *knees*! God! It was horrible—horrible beyond anything I ever dreamed of—to see him groveling there. I supposed, of course, the governor would turn him over to the police. I was all primed for that, and Tate expected it and bawled like a sick calf. But what he said was—what the governor said was, and he said it the way they say 'dust to dust' over a grave—'You poor fool, for such beasts as you the commonwealth has no punishment that wouldn't lighten the load you've got to carry around with you till you die!' That's all there was of it! That's exactly what he said, and can you beat it? I got a room for Tate at the club, and told one of the Japs to put him to bed."

"But the governor had no right," began Ramsay eagerly; "he had no *right*——"

"The king can do no wrong! And, if you fellows don't mind, the incident is closed, and we'll never speak of it again."

WRONG NUMBER

I

THEY called him Wrong Number in the bank because he happened so often and was so annoying. His presence in the White River National was painful to book-keepers, tellers and other practical persons connected with this financial Gibraltar because, without having any definite assignment, he was always busy. He was carried on the rolls as a messenger, though he performed none of the duties commonly associated with the vocation, calling or job of a bank messenger. No one assumed responsibility for Wrong Number, not even the Cashier or the First Vice President, and such rights, powers and immunities as he enjoyed were either self-conferred or were derived from the President, Mr. Webster G. Burgess.

Wrong Number's true appellation as disclosed by the pay-roll was Clarence E. Tibbotts, and the cynical note-teller averred that the initial stood for Elmer. A small, compact figure, fair hair, combed to onion-skin smoothness, a pinkish face and baby blue eyes—there was nothing in Wrong Number's appearance to arouse animosity in any but the stoniest heart. Wrong Number was polite, he was unfailingly cheerful, and when called upon to assist in one place or another he responded with alacrity and no one had reason to complain of his efficiency. He could produce a letter from the files quicker than the regular archivist, or he could play upon the adding machine as though it were an instrument of ten strings. No one had ever taught him anything; no one had the slightest intention of teaching him anything, and yet by imperceptible degrees, he, as a free lance, passed through a period of mild tolerance into acceptance as a valued and useful member of the staff. In the Liberty Loan rushes that wellnigh swamped the department, Wrong Number knew the answers to all the questions that were fired through the wickets. Distracted ladies who had lost their receipts for the first payment and timidly reported this fact found Wrong Number patient and helpful. An early fear in the cages that the president had put Wrong Number into the bank as a spy upon the clerical force was dispelled, when it became known that the young man did on several occasions, conceal or connive at concealing some of those slight errors and inadvertencies that happen in the best regulated of banks. Wrong Number was an enigma, an increasing mystery, nor was he without his enjoyment of his associates' mystification.

Wrong Number's past, though veiled in mist in the White River National, may here be fully and truthfully disclosed. To understand Wrong Number one must also understand Mr. Webster G. Burgess, his discoverer and patron. In addition to being an astute and successful banker, Mr. Burgess owned a string of horses and sent them over various circuits at the usual seasons, and he owned a stock farm of high repute as may be learned by reference to any of the authoritative stud books. If his discreet connection with the race track encouraged the belief that Mr. Burgess was what is vulgarly termed a "sport," his prize-winning shorthorns in conjunction with his generous philanthropies did much to minimize the sin of the racing stable.

Mr. Burgess "took care of his customers," a heavenly attribute in any banker, and did not harass them unnecessarily. Other bankers in town who passed the plate every Sunday in church and knew nothing of Horse might be suspicious and nervous and even disagreeable in a pinch, but Mr. Burgess's many admirers believed that he derived from his association with Horse a breadth of vision and an optimism peculiarly grateful to that considerable number of merchants and manufacturers who appreciate a liberal line of credit. Mr. Burgess was sparing of language and his "Yes" and "No" were equally pointed and final. Some of his utterances, such as a warning to the hand-shaking Vice-president, "Don't bring any anemic people into my office," were widely quoted in business circles. "This is a bank, not the sheriff's office," he remarked to a customer who was turning a sharp corner. "I've told the boys to renew your notes. Quit sobbing and get back on your job."

It was by reason of their devotion to Horse that Burgess and Wrong Number met and knew instantly that the fates had ordained the meeting. Wrong Number had grown up in the equine atmosphere of Lexington—the Lexington of the Blue Grass, and his knowledge of the rest of the world was gained from his journeys to race meets with specimens of the horse kind. Actors are not more superstitious than horsemen and from the time he became a volunteer assistant to the stablemen on the big horse farm the superstition gained ground among the *cognoscenti* that the wings of the Angel of Good Luck had brushed his tow head and that he was a mascot of superior endowment. As he transferred his allegiance from one stable to another luck followed him, and when he picked, one year, as a

Derby winner the unlikeliest horse on the card and that horse galloped home an easy winner, weird and uncanny powers were attributed to Wrong Number.

Burgess had found him sitting on an upturned pail in front of the stable that housed "Lord Templeton" at six o'clock of the morning of the day the stallion strode away from a brilliant field and won an enviable prestige for the Burgess stables. Inspired by Wrong Number's confidence, Burgess had backed "Lord Templeton" far more heavily than he had intended and as a result was enabled to credit a small fortune to his horse account. For four seasons the boy followed the Burgess string and in winter made himself useful on the Burgess farm somewhere north of the Ohio. He showed a genius for acquiring information and was cautious in expressing opinions; he was industrious in an unobtrusive fashion; and he knew about all there is to know about the care and training of horses. Being a prophet he saw the beginning of the end of the Horse Age and sniffed gasoline without resentment, and could take an automobile to pieces and put it together again. Burgess was his ideal of a gentleman, a banker, and a horseman, and he carried his idolatry to the point of imitating his benefactor in manner, dress and speech. Finding that Wrong Number was going into town for a night course in a business college, Burgess paid the bill, and seeing that Wrong Number at twenty-two had outgrown Horse and aspired to a career in finance, Burgess took him into the bank with an injunction to the cashier to "turn him loose in the lot."

While Mrs. Burgess enjoyed the excitement and flutter of grandstands, her sense of humor was unequal to a full appreciation of the social charm of those gentlemen who live in close proximity to Horse. Their ways and their manners and their dialect did not in fact amuse her, and she entertained an utterly unwarranted suspicion that they were not respectable. It was with the gravest doubts and misgivings that she witnessed the rise of Wrong Number who, after that young gentleman's transfer to the bank, turned up in the Burgess town house rather frequently and had even adorned her table.

On an occasion Web had wired her from Chicago that he couldn't get home for a certain charity concert which she had initiated and suggested that she commandeer Wrong Number as an escort; and as no other man of her acquaintance was able or willing to represent the shirking Webster, she did in fact utilize Wrong Number. She was obliged to confess that he had been of the greatest assistance to her and that but for his prompt and vigorous action the programmes, which had not been delivered at the music hall, would never have been recovered from the theatre to which an erring messenger had carried them. Wrong Number, arrayed in evening dress, had handed her in and out of her box and made himself agreeable to three other wives of tired business men who loathed concerts and pleaded important business engagements whenever their peace was menaced by classical music. Mrs. Burgess's bitterness toward Webster for his unaccountable interest in Wrong Number was abated somewhat by these circumstances though she concealed the fact and berated him for his desertion in an hour of need.

Webster G. Burgess was enormously entertained by his wife's social and philanthropic enterprises and he was proud of her ability to manage things. Their two children were away at school and at such times as they dined alone at home the table was the freest confessional for her activities. She never understood why Webster evinced so much greater interest and pleasure in her reports of the warring factions than in affairs that moved smoothly under her supreme direction.

"You know, Web," she began on an evening during the progress of the Great War, after watching her spouse thrust his fork with satisfaction into a pudding she had always found successful in winning him to an amiable mood; "you know, Web, that Mrs. Gurley hasn't the slightest sense of fitness,—no tact,—no delicacy!"

"You've hinted as much before," said Webster placidly. "Cleaned you up in a club election?"

"Web!" ejaculated Mrs. Burgess disdainfully. "You know perfectly well she was completely snowed under at the Women's Civic League election. Do you think after all I did to start that movement I'd let such a woman take the presidency away from me? It isn't that I *cared* for it; heaven knows I've got enough to do without that!"

"Right!" affirmed Burgess readily. "But what's she put over on you now?"

Mrs. Burgess lifted her head quickly from a scrutiny of the percolator flame.

"Put over! Don't you think I give her any chance to put anything over! I wouldn't have her *think* for a minute that she was in any sense a *rival*."

"No; nothing vulgar and common like that," agreed Webster.

"But that woman's got the idea that she's going to entertain all the distinguished people that come here. And the Gurleys have only been here two years and we've lived here all our lives! It's nothing to me, of course, but you know there *is* a certain dignity in being an old family, even here, and my great grandfather was a pioneer governor, and yours was the first State treasurer and that ought to count and always *has* counted. And the Gurleys made all their money out of tomatoes and pickles in a few years; and since they came to town they've just been *forcing* themselves everywhere."

"I'd hardly say that," commented Burgess. "There's no stone wall around this town. I was on a committee of the Chamber of Commerce that invited Gurley to move his canning factory here."

"And after that he was brazen enough to take his account to the Citizen's!" exclaimed Mrs. Burgess.

"That wasn't altogether Gurley's fault, Gertie," replied Burgess, softly.

"You don't mean, Web——"

"I mean that we could have had his account if we'd wanted it."

"Well, I'm glad we're under no obligations to carry them round."

"We're not, if that's the way you see it. But Mrs. Gurley wears pretty good clothes," he suggested, meditatively removing the wrapper from his cigar.

"Webster Burgess, you don't *mean*——"

"I mean that she's smartly set up. You've got to hand it to her, particularly for hats."

"You never see what I wear! You haven't paid the slightest attention to anything I've worn for ten years! You ought to be ashamed of yourself! That woman buys all her clothes in New York, every stitch and feather, and they cost five times what I spend! With the war going on, I don't feel that it's *right* for a woman

to spread herself on clothes. You know you said yourself we ought to economize, and I discharged Marie
and cut down the household bills. Marie was worth
the fifty dollars a month I paid her for the cleaner's
bills she saved me."

Mrs. Burgess was at all times difficult to tease, and
Webster was conscious that he had erred grievously in
broaching the matter of Mrs. Gurley's apparel, which
had never interested him a particle. He listened hum-
bly as Mrs. Burgess gave a detailed account of her
expenditures for raiment for several years, and revealed
what she had never meant to tell him, that out of her
personal allowance she was caring for eight French
orphans in addition to the dozen she had told him
about.

"Well, you're a mighty fine girl, Gertie. You know
I think so."

The tears in Mrs. Burgess's eyes made necessary some
more tangible expression of his affection than this, so
he walked round and kissed her, somewhat to the con-
sternation of the butler who at that moment appeared to clear the table.

"As to money," he continued when they had reached
the living-room, "I got rid of some stock I thought was
a dead one the other day and I meant to give you a
couple of thousand. You may consider it's yours for
clothes or orphans or anything you like."

She murmured her gratitude as she took up her
knitting but he saw that the wound caused by his
ungallant reference to Mrs. Gurley's wardrobe had not
been healed by a kiss and two thousand dollars. Ger-
trude Burgess was a past mistress of the art of
extracting from any such situation its fullest potentialities of compensation. And Webster knew as

he fumbled the evening newspaper that before he departed for the meeting of the War Chest Committee that demanded his presence downtown at eight o'clock he must make it easy for her to pour out her latest grievances against Mrs. Gurley. He is a poor husband who hasn't learned the value of the casual approach. To all outward appearances he had forgotten Mrs. Gurley and for that matter Mrs. Burgess as well when, without looking up from the Government estimate of the winter wheat acreage, he remarked with a perfectly-feigned absent air:

"By the way, Gertie, you started to say something about that Gurley woman. Been breaking into your fences somewhere?"

"If I thought you would be interested, Web——"

This on both sides was mere routine, a part of the accepted method, the established technique of mollification.

"Of course I want to hear it," said Webster, throwing the paper down and planting himself at ease before her with his back to the fire.

"I don't want you to think me unkind or unjust, Web, but there are *some* things, you know!"

He admitted encouragingly that there were indeed some things and bade her go on.

"Well, what made me very indignant was the way that woman walked off with the Italian countess who was here last week to speak to our Red Cross workers. You know I wired Senator Saybrook to extend an invitation to the Countess to come to our house, and he wrote me that he had called on her at the Italian Embassy and she had accepted; and then when the Countess came and I went to the station to meet her, Mrs. Gurley was there all dressed up and carried her off to her house. For sheer impudence, Web, that beat anything I ever heard of. Every one *knows* our home is always open and it had been in the papers that we were to entertain the Countess Paretti. It was not only a reflection on me, Web, but on you as well. And of course the poor Countess wasn't to blame, with all the hurry and confusion at the station, and she didn't know me from Adam; and Mrs. Gurley simply captured her—it was really a case of the most shameless kidnapping—and hurried her into her limousine and took her right off to her house."

"Well, after the time you'd spent thinking up Italian dishes for the lady to consume, I should say that the spaghetti was on us," said Burgess, recalling with relief that the Countess' failure to honor his home had released him for dinner with a British aviator who had proved to be a very amusing and interesting person. "I meant to ask you how the Gurleys got into the sketch. It was a contemptible thing to do, all right. No wonder you're bitter about it. I'll cheerfully punch Gurley's head if that'll do any good."

"What I've been thinking about, Web, is this," said Mrs. Burgess, meditatively. "You know there's an Illyrian delegation coming to town, a special envoy of some of the highest civil and military officials of poor war-swept Illyria. And I heard this afternoon that the Gurleys mean to carry them all to their house for luncheon when the train arrives Thursday at noon just before Governor Eastman receives them at the statehouse, where there's to be a big public meeting. The Gurleys have had their old congressman from Taylorville extend the invitation in Washington and of course the Illyrians wouldn't *know*, Web."

"They would not," said Webster. "The fame of our

domestic cuisine probably hasn't reached Illyria and the delegation would be sure to form a low opinion of Western victualing if they feed at the Gurleys. The Gurleys probably think it a chance to open up a new market for their well-known Eureka brand of catsup in Illyria after the war."

"Don't be absurd!" admonished Mrs. Burgess.

"I'm not absurd; I'm indignant," Webster averred. "Put your cards on the table and let's have a look. What you want to do, Gertie, is to hand the Gurleys one of their own sour pickles. I sympathize fully with your ambition to retaliate. I'll go further than that," he added with a covert glance at the clock; "I'll see what I can do to turn the trick!"

"I don't see *how* it can be done without doing something we can't stoop to do," replied Mrs. Burgess with a hopeful quaver in her voice.

"We must do no stooping," Webster agreed heartily. "It would be far from us to resort to the coarse kidnapping tactics of the Gurleys. And of course you can't go to the mat with Mrs. Gurley in the trainshed. A rough and tumble scrap right there before the Illyrians would be undignified and give 'em a quaint notion of the social habits of the corn belt. But gently and firmly to guide the Illyrian commissioners to our humble home, throw them a luncheon, show 'em the family album and after the show at the statehouse give 'em a whirl to the art institute, and walk 'em through the Illyrian relief rooms, where a pretty little Illyrian girl dressed in her native costume would hand 'em flowers— that's the ticket."

"Oh, Web, you are always so helpful when you want to be! That's the most beautiful idea about the flowers. And perhaps a *group* of Illyrian children would do some folk dances! I'm sure the visitors would be deeply touched by that."

"It would certainly make a hit," said Webster, feeling that he was once more rehabilitated in his wife's affections and confidence. "You say the Gurleys' publicity agent has already gazetted their hospitable designs? Excellent! The more advance work they do on the job the better. We'll give a jar to the pickles—that's the game! Did you get that, Gertie? Pickles, a jar of pickles; a jar to the pickle industry?"

"I was thinking," said Mrs. Burgess, with a far-away look in her eyes, "how charming the folk dances would be and I must see the settlement house superintendent about choosing just the *right* children. But, Web, is it *posssible* to do this so *no one* will know?"

"Don't worry about that," he assured her. "Arrange your luncheon and do it right. I've heard somewhere that a great delicacy in Illyria is broiled grasshoppers, or maybe it's centipedes. Better look that up to be sure not to poison our faithful ally. You'd better whisper to Mrs. Eastman that you'll want the Governor, but tell her it's to meet a prison reformer or a Congo missionary; Eastman is keen on those lines. And ask a few pretty girls and look up the Illyrian religion and get a bishop to suit."

"But you haven't told me how you *mean* to do it, Web. Of course we must be careful——"

"Careful!" repeated Burgess shaking himself into his top coat in the hall door. "My name is discretion. You needn't worry about that part of it! The whole business will be taken care of; dead or alive you shall have the Illyrians."

II

Wrong Number, locked up in the directors' room of
the White River National, studied timetables and maps
and newspaper clippings bearing upon the Western
pilgrimage of the Illyrian Commission. In fifty words
Webster G. Burgess had transferred to his shoulders
full responsibility for producing the Illyrians in the
Burgess home, warning him it must be done with all
dignity and circumspection.

"That's for expenses," said Burgess, handing him
a roll of bills. "This job isn't a bank transaction—
you get me? It's strictly a social event."

Wrong Number betrayed no perturbation as the
president stated the case. Matters of delicacy had
been confided to him before by his patron—the study
of certain horses he thought of buying and wished
an honest report on, the cautious sherlocking of a
country-town customer who was flying higher than his
credit; the disposal of the stock of an automobile dealer
whose business had jumped ahead of his capital;
—such tasks as these Wrong Number had performed to
the entire satisfaction of his employer.

In a new fall suit built by Burgess's tailor, with a
green stripe instead of a blue to differentiate it from the
president's latest, and with a white carnation in his
lapel (Mrs. Burgess provided a pink one for Web every
morning), Wrong Number brooded over this new
problem for two days before he became a man of action.

His broad democracy made him a familiar visitor to
cigar stands, billiard parlors, gun stores, soft drink bars
and cheap hotels where one encounters horsemen,
expert trap shooters, pugilists, book-makers, and other
agreeable characters never met in fashionable clubs.

After much thought he chose as his co-conspirator, Peterson, a big Swede, to whom he had advanced money with which to open a Turkish bath. As the bath was flourishing the Swede welcomed an opportunity to express his gratitude to one he so greatly admired; and besides he still owed Wrong Number two hundred dollars.

"I want a coupla guys that will look right in tall hats," said Wrong Number. "You'll do for one; you'll make up fine for the Illyrian Minister of Foreign Affairs, —he's a tall chap, you'll see from that picture of the bunch being received at the New York city hall. Then you want a little weazened cuss who won't look like an undertaker in a frock coat to stand for the Minister of Finance. We need four more to complete the string and they gotta have uniforms. Comic opera hats with feathers—you can't make 'em too fancy."

The Swede nodded. The Uniform Rank of the Order of the Golden Buck of which he was a prominent member could provide the very thing.

"And I gotta have one real Illyrian to spout the language to the delegation."

"What's the matter with Bensaris who runs a candy shop near where I live? He's the big squeeze among 'em."

"We'll go down and see him. Remember, he don't need to know anything; just do what I tell him. There's a hundred in this for you, Pete, if you pull it right; expenses extra."

"The cops might pinch us," suggested Peterson, warily. "And what you goin' to do about the Mayor? It says in the papers that the Mayor meets the outfit at the Union Station."

"If the cops ask the countersign tell 'em you turned

out to meet the remains of a deceased brother. And
don't worry about the Mayor. He's been over the
Grand Circuit with me and brought his money home
in a trunk."

He drew a memorandum book from his pocket and
set down the following items:

Pete. 2 silk hats; five uni.
Band.
Bensaris.
Mayor.
5 touring cars.

"The honor, it is too much!" pleaded Bensaris when
Wrong Number and Peterson told him all it was
necessary for him to know, at a little table in the rear
of his shop. "But in the day's paper my daughter read
me their excellencies be met at the Union Station;
the arrange' have been change'?"

"The papers are never right," declared Wrong Number. "And you don't need to tell 'em anything."

"A lady, Mees Burgett, she came here to arrange all
Illyrians go to Relief office to sing the songs of my
country. My daughter, she shall dance and hand
flowers to their excellencies!" cried Bensaris beaming.

"The Bensaris family will be featured right through
the bill," said Wrong Number.

"It is too kind," insisted Bensaris. "It is for the
Mayor you make the arrange'?"

"I represent the financial interests of our city,"
Wrong Number replied. "You want to go the limit
in dressing up the automobiles; make 'em look like
Fourth o' July in your native O'Learyo. Where do
we doll 'em up, Pete?"

A garage of a friend in the next block would serve

admirably and Peterson promised to co-operate with Bensaris in doing the job properly.

"Tail coat and two gallon hat for Mr. Bensaris," said Wrong Number. "Pete, you look after that." He pressed cash upon Mr. Bensaris and noted the amount in his book. "We'll call it a heat," he said, and went up town to pilot Mr. Webster G. Burgess to a ten round match for points between two local amateurs that was being pulled off behind closed doors in an abandoned skating rink.

III

The Illyrian Commission had just breakfasted when their train reached Farrington on the State line, where the Mayor of the capital city, Mr. Clarence E. Tibbotts, *alias* Wrong Number, and Mr. Zoloff Bensaris, all in shining hats, boarded the train.

Having studied the portraits of the distinguished Illyrians in a Sunday supplement provided by Mr. Tibbotts, Mr. Bensaris effected the introductions without an error, and having been carefully coached by the same guide he did not handle his two-gallon hat as though it were a tray of chocolate sundaes. The kindness of the mayor and his associates in coming so far to meet the Commission deeply touched the visitors. The Fourth Assistant Secretary of State, who was doing the honors of the American government, heard without emotion of the slight changes in the programme.

"We thought the Commission would be tired of the train," explained Wrong Number, who was relieved to find that his cutaway was of the same vintage as the Fourth Assistant Secretary's; "so we get off at the first stop this side of town and motor in."

"Luncheon at Mr. Gurley's," said the Secretary, consulting a sheaf of telegrams.

"Had to change that, too," said Wrong Number carelessly; "they have scarlet fever at the Gurleys. The Webster G. Burgesses will throw the luncheon."

The Secretary made a note of the change and thrust his papers into his pocket. Mr. Tibbotts handed round his cigarette case, a silver trinket bearing "Lord Templeton's" head in enamel relief, a Christmas gift from Mr. Webster G. Burgess, and joined in a discussion of the morning's news from the Balkans, where the Illyrian troops were acquitting themselves with the highest credit.

When the suburban villas of Ravenswood began to dance along the windows, Mr. Tibbotts marshaled his party and as they stepped from the private car a band struck up the Illyrian national hymn. Several dozen students from the nearby college who chanced to be at the station raised a cheer. As the Illyrians were piloted across the platform to the fleet of waiting automobiles, the spectators were interested in the movements of another party,—a party fully as distinguished in appearance—that emerged from the station and tripped briskly into a sleeper farther along in the train that had discharged the Illyrians. Here, too, were silk hats upon two sober-looking gentlemen who could hardly be other than statesmen, and uniforms of great splendor upon five stalwart forms, with topping plumes waving blithely in the autumn air. And out of the corner of his eye Mr. Clarence E. Tibbotts, just seating himself in a big touring car, between the Fourth Assistant Secretary of State and the Illyrian Minister of Finance, saw Peterson's work, and knew that it was good.

The procession swept into town at a lively clip, set by the driver of the first car, that bore the Mayor and the Minister of Foreign Affairs, which was driven by a victor of many motor speed trials carefully chosen by Wrong Number for this important service. The piquant flavor of Wrong Number's language as he pointed out objects of interest amused the American Secretary, much bored in his pilgrimages by the solemnities of reception committees, and it served also to convince the Illyrian Minister of Finance of the inadequacy of his own English.

Lusty cheering greeted the party as it moved slowly through the business district. When the Illyrian Minister and the Fourth Secretary lifted their hats Wrong Number kept time with them; he enjoyed lifting his hat. He enjoyed also a view of half a dozen clerks on the steps of the White River National, who cheered deliriously as they espied their associate and hastened within to spread the news of his latest exploit through the cages.

It is fortunate that Mr. Tibbotts had taken the precaution to plant a motion-picture camera opposite the Burgess home, for otherwise the historical student of the future might be puzzled to find that the first edition of the *Evening Journal* of that day showed the Illyrian delegation passing through the gates of the Union Station, with a glimpse of Mrs. Arnold D. Gurley handing a large bouquet of roses to a tall gentleman who was not in fact the Illyrian Minister of Foreign Affairs but the proprietor of Peterson's bath parlors. The *Journal* suppressed its pictures in later editions, thereby saving its face, and printed without illustrations an excellent account of the reception of the Illyrians at Ravenswood and of the luncheon, from facts furnished by Mr. Tibbotts, who stood guard at

the door of the Burgess home while the function was
in progress in the dining room.

Who ate Mrs. Gurley's luncheon is a moot question
in the select circles of the capital city. Peterson and
his party might have enjoyed the repast had not the
proprietor of the bath parlors, after accepting Mrs.
Gurley's bouquet at the station gates, vanished with
his accomplices in the general direction of their lodge
room of the Order of the Golden Buck.

When foolish reporters tried to learn at the City
Hall why the Mayor had changed without warning
the plans for the reception, that official referred them
to the Secretary of the Chamber of Commerce, who
in turn directed the inquirer's to the Governor's office
and the Governor, having been properly admonished
by his wife, knew nothing whatever about it.

IV

As the Burgesses were reviewing the incidents of the
day at dinner that evening, Mrs. Burgess remarked
suddenly,

"Now that it's all over, Web, do you think it was
quite fair, really *right?*"

"You mean," asked Webster, huskily, "that you're
not satisfied with the way it was handled?"

"Oh, not that! But it was almost *too* complete; and
poor Mrs. Gurley must be horribly humiliated."

"Crushed, I should say," remarked Webster cheerfully. "This ought to hold her for a while."

"But that fake delegation you had at the station to
deceive Mrs. Gurley——"

"I beg your pardon," Webster interrupted, "I assure
you I had nothing to do with it."

"Well, all I *know* is that just before dinner Mrs.
Eastman called me up and said the Governor had just
telephoned her that Mrs. Gurley tried to *kiss* the hand
of some man she took for the Illyrian Minister of
Foreign Affairs as he went through the station gates.
And the man is nothing but a rubber in a Turkish bath.
You *wouldn't* have done that, Web, would you?"

"No, dear, I would not! For one thing, I wouldn't
have been smart enough to think it up."

"And you know, Web, I shouldn't want you to think
me mean and envious and jealous. I'm not really that
way; you know I'm not! And of course if I'd thought
you'd really bring the Illyrians here, I should never
have mentioned it at all."

Webster passed his hand across his brow in bewilderment. At moments when he thought he was meeting
the most exacting requirements of the marital relation-
ship it was enormously disturbing to find himself
defeated.

"Your luncheon was a great success; the talk at the
table was wonderful; and the girls you brought in made
a big hit. It's the best party you ever pulled off," he
declared warmly.

"I'm glad you think so," she said slowly, giving him
her direct gaze across the table, "but there were one
or two things I didn't quite like, Web. It seemed to
me your young friend Tibbotts was a little *too* con-
spicuous. I'm surprised that you let him come to
the house. You couldn't—you *wouldn't* have let him
know how the Illyrians came here? He really seemed
to assume full charge of the party, and in the drawing
room he was flirting outrageously with pretty Lois
Hubbard, and kept her giggling when I'd asked her
specially to be nice to the Fourth Assistant Secretary,

who's a bachelor, you know. And if Mrs. Hubbard *knew* we had introduced Lois to a boy from the race-track——"

"It would be awful," said Webster with one of the elusive grins that always baffled her.

"What would be awful?" she demanded.

"Oh, nothing! I was thinking of Wrong Number and what a blow it would be if I should lose him. I must remember to raise his salary in the morning."

THE END.